OTHER BOOKS IN THE NO PLACE LIKE HOLMES SERIES:

THE FUTURE DOOR

NO PLACE LIKE HOLMES
VOLUME 2

JASON LETHCOE

THOMAS NELSON
Since 1798

NASHVILLE   DALLAS   MEXICO CITY   RIO DE JANEIRO

Published in Nashville, Tennessee, by Tommy Nelson. Tommy Nelson is a trademark of Thomas Nelson, Inc.

Tommy Nelson® titles may be purchased in bulk for educational, business, fund-raising, or sales promotional use. For information, please e-mail SpecialMarkets@ThomasNelson.com.

Scripture quotations are taken from THE NEW KING JAMES VERSION. © 1982 by Thomas Nelson, Inc. Used by permission. All rights reserved.

Library of Congress Cataloging-in-Publication Data

Lethcoe, Jason.
  The future door / Jason Lethcoe.
    p. cm. — (No place like Holmes ; bk. 2)
  Summary: When Charlotte, a long-term fan of Sherlock Holmes, moves into his former apartment on Baker Street then disappears along with a special invention, her neighbors and fellow detectives Griffin and his uncle try to find her in a race against the clock that bends time itself.
  ISBN 978-1-4003-1730-1 (pbk.)
  [1. Missing persons—Fiction. 2. Uncles—Fiction. 3. Inventions—Fiction. 4. Time travel—Fiction. 5. Christian life—Fiction. 6. Characters in literature—Fiction. 7. London (England)—History—19th century—Fiction. 8. Great Britain—History—19th century—Fiction. 9. Mystery and detective stories.] I. Title.
  PZ7.L56647Fut 2011
  [Fic]—dc23

                                                                2011027871

Printed in the United States of America

12 13 14 15 QG 6 5 4 3 2 1

For Nancy
Thank you for your timeless love.
You are my past, my present, and my future.

—J.J.L.

ACKNOWLEDGMENTS

I would like to acknowledge Molly Kempf Hodgin, my longtime editor and partner in crime. Thanks for your vigilance, skill, and unending support. Without your help, Griffin's story surely would have remained untold.

The only reason for time is so that everything doesn't happen at once.

—ALBERT EINSTEIN

CONTENTS

CONTENTS

SEPARATING THE FACTS

It is of particular importance that we stick to the facts when talking about the history of Griffin Sharpe. Although scholars have attributed many fantastic deeds to the World's Most Secret Detective, we must try, if possible, to remain objective and sort out what is fact from fiction.

For example, there are those who say that Griffin Sharpe traveled into outer space, not once, but three times, and that on each voyage he prevented Earth from being destroyed by otherworldly forces. This we know to be true.

And there are those who say that later in life he thwarted a plan by the Nazis to resurrect Adolf Hitler using robotic parts.

This we also know to be true. The account was corroborated by several eyewitnesses.

In the mystery of the Iron Cross, Mr. Sharpe is said to have bested the infamous Red Baron in aerial combat, and in another account he is said to have impersonated both the president of the United States and the prime minister of England in order to save both their lives. Both stories are true.

And I myself have said on a number of occasions that when he was eleven years of age, Griffin Sharpe traveled in a time machine and saved us from a terrible future we never knew existed.

But here we must separate fact from fiction.

While it is most certainly true that he traveled through time and, while doing so, he actually became the first person in history to have tea with himself, I have been contacted by Dame Victoria Sharpe regarding this incident, and she has informed me that on one important fact I am gravely mistaken.

Griffin Sharpe was actually *twelve* years old when it happened, not eleven. I apologize, dear reader, for this terrible error. And let me assure you that everything you are about to read from this point onward was carefully researched.

Now then, since the writing of my first book about Mr. Sharpe, *No Place Like Holmes*, I have been inundated with letters from Griffin Sharpe fans begging to know more of the great detective's exploits. But the real challenge for me was, which one to choose? For as you know, Mr. Sharpe has done so many incredible things that each account makes for an interesting story.

But after spending many sleepless nights researching his cases, I finally decided that none is quite as remarkable as the one you are about to read.

So please pull up a chair and get your tea and scones, for once again we're about to travel into the past. As the years fly behind us, we shall follow Griffin Sharpe as he travels forward in time, embarking on this strange adventure, and meeting us in the most unlikely of places . . . the future!

We shall stick to the facts as they actually happened. Or, should I say, are about to happen.

JASON LETHCOE

MARCH 2011

PROLOGUE

Mrs. Hudson wiped her hands on her apron as she hurried to the front door of 221 Baker Street. The delicious scent of roasting chicken and rosemary wafted behind her as she rushed out of the kitchen to answer the persistent knocking.

"Half a moment," she called irritably. If there was one thing she didn't like, it was being interrupted when she was in the middle of preparing a meal for her tenants. After pausing to tuck a few stray hairs beneath her cap, she opened the door. To her surprise, a pretty young woman dressed in boys' clothing was standing on the doorstep.

"May I help you?" Mrs. Hudson asked suspiciously. She scanned the woman's attire, taking in her dyed wool jacket, checked trousers, and newsboy cap. Somehow, in spite of the unflattering clothing, the girl still managed to look feminine.

"You must be Mrs. Hudson! My name is Charlotte Pepper. It's so very nice to meet you," she said, extending her hand. Mrs. Hudson was taken aback for a moment, but then, seeing no other polite way around it, shook Charlotte's offered hand.

"Ouch!" said Mrs. Hudson, releasing Miss Pepper's grip. The ring the young lady wore was quite sharp.

"Oh! Please forgive me," said Charlotte Pepper, and quickly removed the ring. "I didn't mean to injure you. Sometimes I forget I have that old ring on."

"And what can I do for you, Miss Pepper?" Mrs. Hudson asked impatiently.

"I heard that you were looking for a new tenant and have come to inquire about the apartment. How much rent do you require?"

Mrs. Hudson noticed that when she spoke, Charlotte Pepper didn't make eye contact, but instead glanced everywhere else, including the hallway behind her.

A smile played around the young woman's full lips, and her huge brown eyes danced with excitement. Turning back to the landlady, she asked, "Is it indeed the former residence of the famous Sherlock Holmes?"

"Until recently, yes," Mrs. Hudson replied with a sigh. Ever since her favorite tenant had departed, she'd had no end of "lookie-loos" showing up, wanting to catch a glimpse of the great detective's apartment.

"Wonderful! May I see it?" said Charlotte Pepper.

"Young lady," Mrs. Hudson said. "I don't wish to be rude, but the apartment in question is quite expensive." She glanced at the young woman's shabby clothing. "Mr. Holmes was an accomplished detective with a reliable income, and I mean for my new tenant to meet the same qualifications."

If Charlotte Pepper was offended by the remark, she didn't show it.

"Well, I assure you that money is no object," she stated. "Simply name your price and I shall pay it."

Mrs. Hudson started to reply, but Charlotte interrupted her, holding up a finger.

"I am absolutely without question the biggest fan of Sherlock Holmes who ever lived. I am a bit of an amateur detective myself and will treat the premises with the utmost care and respect. I am clean, decent, and well-mannered. In other words, I am the perfect tenant. I'm sure we'll get along famously."

She reached into her jacket pocket and removed the largest amount of British currency Mrs. Hudson had ever seen one person carry. After pressing it into the startled landlady's hand, she stepped past her into the hallway.

"I believe my new rooms are right up these stairs, correct?"

Mrs. Hudson, feeling completely flummoxed, watched as the young woman charged down the hall and up the stairs. *Another detective at Baker Street?* she thought. First there was Mr. Holmes, then Mr. Snodgrass, and now this precocious female? And just who did Charlotte Pepper think she was, bossing her around, not asking but *telling* her that she was to accept her as her tenant?

But Mrs. Hudson didn't express her feelings aloud. For one of the first times in her life, the landlady was left absolutely speechless. She felt quite dazed by Miss Pepper's presence and persuasive speech, and decided that it was easier to comply with the woman's demands than to resist. And she couldn't help but think that her old tenant, Mr. Sherlock Holmes, would have enjoyed seeing that happen for once.

If only he were still here, she thought sadly.

Mrs. Hudson respected that Mr. Holmes had finally moved to Sussex to live a quiet life of retirement, but his absence at Baker Street was a loss that she felt deeply. And without Sherlock

Holmes's lanky figure patrolling the streets of London, the world felt much more dangerous. Even though Mr. Snodgrass and Master Sharpe had proven that they were capable detectives and lived next door, it just wasn't the same. In her opinion, the boy and his uncle were "second best," and that just wasn't good enough.

She felt quite light-headed as she closed the front door, and failed to notice the disreputable character who was standing beneath the gaslight on the opposite side of the street. The huge man watched her with a twisted grin.

Right on schedule, he thought.

Then he reached up to the gaslight and opened one of the glass panes. After removing two small pieces of paper from a tiny metal box, he closed the pane again almost silently. Then, with hardly a backward glance, the man hurried into the shadows.

THE MISSING SPYGLASS

G riffin Sharpe clutched his ebony walking stick, fight-
ing to keep his balance as the steamship rocked back
and forth on the churning waves. The storm had
forced most of the passengers below, but not him.

His leg was still sore from where it had been permanently
injured in a battle with one of the most evil men in London. But
he didn't complain about the discomfort. Instead, he gritted his
teeth and leaned more heavily on his stick, forcing himself to
limp along the slippery rail to the bow of the heaving ship.

Twenty life preservers, three lanterns, one shuffleboard stick . . .
Griffin silently counted the things he saw as he hobbled forward, a longtime habit that helped him cope with anxiety or
discomfort. He fought down his feeling of seasickness and
forced himself to focus on the task at hand.

Griffin Sharpe's mind was a constant fireworks display of
thoughts and ideas, and there were very few people like him.
His unique reasoning and deductive abilities were gifts from
heaven, and Griffin intended to use them in the service of
others. Right now, he was helping the captain of the ship find

his favorite spyglass, which had mysteriously disappeared. The captain had always kept it in his private chambers, and earlier that afternoon, when he'd gone to retrieve it, he discovered that the small telescope had vanished.

His leg was really throbbing, and the doctor had warned him that he needed to treat it gently, but Griffin couldn't help himself. Trifling things like unpleasant weather and rollicking waves wouldn't stop him when he was feeling excited to solve a mystery.

And as the twelve-year-old detective hobbled forward, his usually sad, blue eyes were alight with excitement, for Griffin knew he was getting close to cracking the case, and nothing thrilled him more than that.

He ignored the cold spray that had thoroughly soaked through his tweed jacket and cap as he searched everything near the front of the ship. After several long minutes, he finally spotted what he was looking for. A few feet to the left of a life preserver, right at the top of the bow, was a tiny, glittering object wedged between the deck plates.

He wiped his magnifying glass on his damp shirt and bent closer so that he could see the object better.

It was a tiny brass ring.

But Griffin could tell right away that it wasn't the kind of ring that was to be worn on a finger as a piece of jewelry. He studied it closely, noticing the small threads that wound around inside the circular band and the small bit of glass in its center.

The boy knew the ring was a piece of a brass telescope, the eyepiece that was supposed to be attached to the observing end.

He wedged the small ring out of the plates with his penknife and placed it carefully in his pocket. Then he smiled and wiped the salty mist from his forehead with his sleeve.

Now that he'd found this clue, Griffin had a pretty good idea of who had taken the captain's favorite brass telescope and what had happened to it. All that was left for him to do was to gather one more piece of evidence to prove that his hunch was correct. He swayed with the rolling ship as he limped to the door that led back inside the ship's main cabin.

Tap-tap-tap went his stick as it hit the weathered planks. Griffin studied the deck in front of him as he walked. The marks he followed were a nearly invisible series of small, gray half-moons that led from the bow back to the inside of the ship.

Nobody else would have observed what the marks were, but Griffin could tell that they were made by the heel of someone's shoe, someone who had stepped briefly into a puddle of grease.

He knew it to be grease because the rain and the waves weren't washing the marks away. Instead, droplets of water gathered in each half-moon and glittered in the ship's lamplight. Oil and water didn't mix. And Griffin had his suspicions as to where this particular kind of grease had originated. Like a young bloodhound, he was following the trail back to its point of origin.

Thirteen, fourteen, fifteen . . . He automatically counted the tracks as he entered the inside of the ship and followed the trail up a winding staircase. But this time, his habitual counting couldn't distract him from the pain in his leg, which had begun to burn so badly that he finally had to stop and sit on the uppermost stair.

As he massaged his calf, he glanced at the sumptuously

decorated hallway in front of him. He was now on the upper deck, where the captain and the first-class passengers had their quarters.

Velvet curtains with silver tassels framed the hallway entrance, and curling filigree decorated the shiny brass portholes. Mounted on the wall opposite from where he sat was a small oil painting. It was a picture of the Westminster Clock Tower, the famous clock that many people called Big Ben.

Flashes of memory, like photographs, raced through his mind as he stared at the painting.

Two tons of stolen fireworks wrapped in unusual red paper. A gigantic submarine that looked like the Loch Ness monster. Lightning-fast railway cars of a futuristic design. The Westminster Tower, the same one as in the painting, turned into the world's largest time bomb . . .

The memories from his last adventure played through his mind as if he were watching a magic lantern show.

But there was one memory that plagued him worst of all. As hard as he tried, he would never be able to forget the cruel face of Nigel Moriarty. The terrible man was cousin to the infamous Professor Moriarty, Sherlock Holmes's archenemy, and his face constantly haunted Griffin's dreams.

Griffin could picture him even now, and just the thought of him made the hair on the back of his neck stand on end. He felt his hands go clammy as he thought of Nigel's neat, curled mustache and his terrible laugh—the laugh that had filled his ears as the villain had plunged a sword into Griffin's back.

That cruel blow had happened at the precise moment when Griffin had used one of his uncle's inventions to defuse the gigantic time bomb that would have destroyed half of London.

Griffin reached over and took his ebony walking stick from where it was leaning against the banister and laid it carefully across his knees. Then, with a sick feeling in his stomach, he grasped the silver top, a knob with the engraved letters *N.M.* on it, and pulled outward while holding firmly to the wooden shaft.

A few inches of shiny steel slid out from inside the cane.

He stared down at the partially revealed blade. It had been this very sword, the one that was hidden inside the stick he now used as a crutch, that had nearly ended his life.

As he turned the weapon in his hand, Griffin's sad eyes were reflected in the weapon's mirror-like surface. It seemed an eternity ago since he'd boarded a similar boat and then a train that had brought him to London and had changed his life forever.

Griffin had arrived in London at the beginning of the summer to spend his vacation with his uncle, whom he had mistakenly thought was the famous detective Sherlock Holmes. But he'd soon found out that his uncle was not Holmes, but instead merely shared a hallway with him, with his uncle living at 221A Baker Street, and Holmes living at 221B.

After arriving, Griffin and his persnickety uncle had gotten off to a bad start. Rupert Snodgrass was a would-be detective who had been living so long in Sherlock Holmes's shadow that life had turned him bitter. And prior to Griffin's arrival, Snodgrass hadn't been able to secure a single case and had been nearly evicted from his apartment.

But when Griffin brought a desperate woman who claimed the Loch Ness monster had eaten her husband to his uncle for help, the boy and his uncle had formed a temporary alliance to help solve the unlikely mystery.

And to Rupert's and Griffin's surprise, they found that by working together they had proved to be a remarkable team.

Yet, although they had solved the case, it had not been without consequences. Griffin had nearly died when Nigel Moriarty had stabbed him in the back with the sword, and he'd also suffered the injury to his leg that had left him with his permanent limp.

But if there was one thing that his father had taught him, it was that there was always a silver lining. Griffin's dad was a Methodist minister, and believed that God could use even the most painful tragedies for good. The "good," as Griffin understood it, was that as a result of almost losing his nephew, Rupert Snodgrass had discovered that he actually cared for Griffin and that having family was more important than besting his rival, Sherlock Holmes. And against what had seemed impossible odds, Griffin and his uncle now shared a close friendship.

And the silver lining for Griffin Sharpe was actually having a friend in his uncle who understood and cared for him. It was something new and wonderful for the shy boy who had always been bullied.

Griffin knocked at the door marked Captain's Quarters. A few moments later he heard a low, rumbling voice call, "Enter!"

As the door of the captain's sumptuously decorated room swung open, Griffin quickly took note of the occupants gathered there. The anxious captain sat at a broad desk, his ruddy features framed by a pair of enormous sideburns.

One of his sideburns is three centimeters higher than the other, Griffin noted. He also noticed a distinct nicotine stain on the right side of the captain's lips, an indication that the captain was a frequent tobacco smoker.

Next to him stood a young boy of about ten, wearing a sailor suit and absently playing with a fountain pen. His clothes were neatly pressed, but Griffin noticed that there were three stray threads on his left sleeve, that the brim of his hat was crumpled, and that his shoes were dirty. A woman sat in a chair against the wall opposite them, shrouded in a black veil and wearing a glittering silver ring on her left hand. Griffin couldn't tell much about her and assumed that she must be a guest of the captain's.

On the other side of the room, sitting in a comfortable leather chair, was a scruffy man wearing a battered brown derby.

As Griffin scanned the room, taking in all the details, a slow smile spread across his face. He glanced over at the scruffy man, who happened to be his uncle Rupert, and gave him a quick nod.

His uncle's features relaxed for the first time since they'd embarked on the urgent journey to Boston. Griffin could tell his uncle knew that he'd solved the case.

But Griffin also knew that this was no time to celebrate. He was too worried about his parents to truly enjoy his victory. The missing telescope had been a welcome diversion from his anxiety, but it hadn't helped the boat move any faster.

And until he solved the greater mystery concerning his parents' disappearance, he would never truly be able to rest.

BOSTON

I f you had used my latest invention, the Snodgrass Radiated Footprint Scanner, you might have had an easier time locating those tracks," Rupert Snodgrass said. He sniffed with self-importance. "However, you seem to have done it anyway, even without my help," he added.

Griffin smiled, thinking about his uncle's incredible engineering skill. Rupert tended to name each of his inventions after himself, calling it the "Snodgrass such and such." And although each of the devices was remarkable and more amazing than anything Griffin ever could have imagined, it seemed that somehow, inevitably, his uncle never got the credit or the fame he desired.

Some of Griffin's favorites were the Snodgrass Lightning Boiler (an electric teapot), the Snodgrass Haberdash Weather Repeller (a hat with a small umbrella sticking out of it), the Snodgrass Super Finder (a machine that found lost metal objects), and his most favorite invention of all, the Snodgrass Mechanized Manservant, which was an actual walking, talking, steam-driven, mechanical man named Watts!

"Now, tell me again, how exactly did you arrive at the conclusion that the captain's son had stolen his favorite spyglass?" Rupert asked.

Griffin hefted his small carpetbag as they made their way down the gangplank. The sights and sounds of Boston Harbor were all around him, and it was a relief to Griffin to finally be back home. He noticed that in one hand his uncle carried a satchel filled with some of his amazing inventions, and in the other he held Toby's leash.

Griffin glanced down at the happy, trotting hound, who seemed to be enjoying the sights and sounds of Boston Harbor as much as he was. The dog was clearly excited to be off the ship at last.

Griffin turned his attention back to his uncle's question.

"Well, it was pretty simple, actually," Griffin said. "First of all, I could tell that whoever had done it was probably someone small. The size of the greasy footprints that led from the engine room suggested that it was a child. That, and while I was in the engine room, I found something else."

Griffin indicated the pocket of his jacket with a tilt of his chin. Sticking out of it was something that looked like a black handkerchief.

He handed it to Rupert, who examined it as they followed the crowd onto the dock. The black cloth bore a rather crude representation of a skull and crossbones in its center.

"I could tell that the person who made this flag had used a particular kind of shoe polish to make it look black, the scent of which is rather distinctive," Griffin said. Rupert gave the cloth an experimental sniff and wrinkled his nose.

"So naturally it made sense that the person I was looking

for was probably a child who was playing pirate and had access to various parts of the ship that others couldn't get into."

"Like the engine room," Rupert said.

"Exactly," Griffin replied. "I then traced the footprints from the engine room to the bow of the ship and found the missing eyepiece. I assumed that the boy had probably gone up there with the spyglass to pretend to look for enemy ships or a desert island."

Griffin and his uncle made their way across the dock, passing row upon row of sailing ships with tall masts. The pungent smell of brine and drying fishing nets was in the air, and because Griffin was so glad to be finally home, it almost, but not quite, smelled like perfume to him. He'd never enjoyed the smell of fish.

Seagulls squawked overhead, scanning the busy docks for any signs of unwanted food. The crowd had thinned as passengers met loved ones and dispersed to waiting carriages. As Rupert and Griffin moved toward a neat row of hansom cabs, Griffin continued with his account.

"Anyway, I assumed that while focusing the telescope, the boy had accidentally unscrewed the eyepiece and lost it when it dropped on deck. Feeling afraid that he would get in trouble with his father, he would have then hidden the telescope somewhere safe or thrown it overboard."

At his uncle's waving gesture, a black cab rolled up the cobblestone streets and stopped in front of them. As the cabbie disembarked and helped them with their luggage, Griffin continued.

"So I just followed the boy's tracks back upstairs to the captain's quarters. When the door opened, I could tell immediately from the scent, the marks of shoe polish on his hands, and the light grease on the heel of his right shoe that it was the captain's son who had taken the spyglass." Griffin shrugged and added humbly, "Not only that, but when I saw the creases in his sailor's cap, I assumed that he'd bent it into a different shape, probably to look like a pirate's hat. It really was pretty simple."

Rupert Snodgrass smirked and shook his head. It was hard to argue with his nephew's brilliance. It was also hard for him to accept the way Griffin reasoned his way through a case. His method of observation and deduction reminded him a lot of his rival, Sherlock Holmes. Even though he and Holmes had patched up their relationship, Rupert felt that he would never get over the sting of always feeling inferior to him.

But he had grown to love his nephew, and even though Griffin's brilliance sometimes made him jealous, he chose to overlook it.

Rupert helped Griffin up into the carriage as the cabbie hoisted their heaviest luggage to the roof of the cab. Then Rupert called Toby, and the hound happily bounded inside, commencing to sniff at the worn leather seats.

Because of his hurt leg, Griffin was still having a difficult time getting in and out of high places. After his uncle helped him into the cab, Griffin sighed with relief as he settled into the seat opposite Rupert. It felt really good to be able to stop walking for a while.

Rupert removed a small leather book from his coat pocket. Griffin recognized it as the journal he always carried. He took out a piece of folded paper—written directions to Griffin's house—and handed it to the cabbie. Then, with a lurch, the cab started forward, and they were soon rattling down the familiar cobblestone streets of Griffin's neighborhood.

Row upon row of beautiful brick buildings passed on either side of them as they wound down the narrow streets. Griffin breathed deeply, appreciating the unique smell of the city. As he gazed out of the carriage window at the shopkeepers with their barrels of fresh apples, cheese, and dried meat, he thought of the many times he and his parents had walked there.

An invisible fist closed around his heart as he thought about them. After the last case, Griffin had received a telegram from someone named John Andover, who had informed them of the terrible news that his parents had been kidnapped! Griffin had his suspicions that Nigel Moriarty was behind the disappearance, and that it was his way of exacting revenge—he just wasn't sure how he planned to do it.

Griffin chewed his thumbnail as he gazed at the familiar Boston streets. He desperately hoped that they could find clues that would lead them to the kidnappers and that his mom and dad were okay. But what he couldn't figure out was why it had happened. If Moriarty was indeed behind this, what did he hope to accomplish by stealing Griffin's parents away?

The boy's thoughts turned to dark things, and he tried desperately not to fear the worst.

Rupert interrupted Griffin's anxious musings. "And how did you know whether the boy had hidden it or thrown it overboard?"

"Hmm?" Griffin replied. His thoughts had been so focused on his parents that he'd almost forgotten what they had been talking about.

"You know, the telescope. Where was it?"

"Oh yes. Well, that part was easy. I simply took one look at the—"

CRACK! An explosion rattled the carriage. Griffin was nearly thrown from his seat as the carriage careened sideways. He looked down and saw that his lap was covered with broken glass.

"What the deuce?" Rupert shouted.

Griffin looked out the shattered window and saw that a second carriage had pulled up next to theirs. The passenger, a black-cloaked figure wearing a broad-brimmed hat and whose eyes were covered by a pair of opaque goggles, was pointing something at their window. Griffin didn't register what it was until it was almost too late!

A Gatling gun! The thought had barely entered Griffin's mind before there was another series of loud *cracks*. Griffin automatically ducked as a round of bullets thudded into the wooden carriage walls behind him.

"Uncle, get down!" Griffin shouted.

Rupert, who was still stunned from the first explosion, was busily brushing glass from his hat and vest. Griffin leapt from his seat and tackled his uncle to the floor.

And it was a good thing he did. The next round of bullets hit the seat right where Rupert's chest had been a fraction of a second earlier.

Toby, who had been sleeping next to Griffin, yelped and dove beneath the seat. The hound whimpered as bullets continued to thump into the splintering wood of the carriage walls.

Griffin felt the carriage lurch forward as the driver whipped the horses to greater speed. "Out of the way!" the cabbie yelled. Bystanders screamed and dove for cover as the cab weaved back and forth through the crowded streets.

Daylight streamed into the cab from a myriad of holes, and

Griffin fancied that he could hear the air whistle through them as they thundered down the road.

With his face pressed to the floor, he had no idea where they were heading or if the shooter was still beside them. He was thankful that the driver hadn't kicked them out of the cab, and assumed that the only reason for this must have been that he was as scared as they were.

"Where's your Stinger, boy?" Rupert shouted from where he crouched beside him.

"What?"

"Your Stinger!" For emphasis, Rupert made the fingers of his right hand into the shape of a gun.

Griffin suddenly remembered what his uncle was talking about. Rupert's inventions ranged from incredible crime-solving devices to futuristic pistols that could fire an array of different ammunitions, including beams of light and different types of plasma. Griffin had been given one of the weapons on their last adventure, a gun called the Snodgrass Stinger that shot an immobilizing green goo at its intended target. With an inward groan, he realized that he'd left it in his carpetbag, which the driver had loaded on top of the carriage.

"I d-don't have it," Griffin stammered. "It's in my bag on the roof!"

The cab made a sharp right turn, and Griffin felt it tilt, the momentum lifting the left wheels entirely off the ground. He and his uncle were thrown across the floor, and Griffin felt his shoulder bang into something hard. The door that he'd hit flung open, and he felt himself sliding out of the carriage.

"Help!" he cried.

His uncle's hand shot out and just managed to grab hold

of Griffin's shoe. The boy dangled outside of the racing cab, hanging upside down with his head poised just inches above the cobblestone street.

Whether it was because of the danger or an increased sense of anxiety, Griffin's mind went into overdrive, processing everything around him with intense clarity as if he were taking a series of photographs.

Two alley cats, one with eyes of green, the other yellow.

Flash!

Shop windows with the names T. Quane, Tanner, Long's Publick House, Saint Hour's Timepieces, and Hopper's Haberdashery.

Flash!

A discarded boot lying next to three barrels of mackerel.

Flash!

A beggar with one eye and no socks.

Flash!

A second carriage with a woman wearing goggles and holding a Gatling gun . . .

And in that unique way that he processed things, Griffin saw for the first time that it wasn't a *man* but a *woman* who pursued them. Her long hair was deep red and streamed from beneath her broad-brimmed hat. She was dressed like a man, wearing not only the industrial goggles he'd seen earlier but a green silk cravat and ruby red waistcoat. Her lips were bloodred, and her perfect rows of white teeth stood out in sharp contrast as she lowered her sights on Griffin and flashed him a malicious grin.

And in that beautiful smile Griffin could see very clearly that he was about to die.

Suddenly, there was a sharp snapping noise. Griffin felt

something attach itself to his coat. Then, without warning, he found himself jerked upward like a marionette on a string.

As a volley of bullets sparked off of the cobblestones where his head had been only seconds earlier, he saw his uncle standing before him with a strange contraption on his wrist. Rupert's legs were braced against the carriage wall for support as a cable spun on a large pulley, reeling Griffin in like a freshly caught fish.

"Got you, boy!" Rupert shouted as he yanked Griffin back into the cab.

Griffin's relief was only momentary. He was just about to warn his uncle to get down, for the woman in the next cab was sure to have reloaded. But the words never left his mouth. The next thing he knew, the cab that they were riding in gave a sudden, tremendous lurch.

There was a terrific *BOOM!*

And as his head collided against something solid, everything went black.

THE MORIARTYS

The beefy man hesitated before knocking on the carved wooden door. His tiny eyes were glazed over in concentration, and his big jaw worked up and down, chewing a piece of stale licorice.

Chester Drummond was not an intelligent man; anybody could tell that by looking at him. But he was good at following orders . . . when he could remember them.

And as Chester stood outside the door of the most feared man in London, he desperately tried to remember what he had wanted to say.

Chester twisted his floppy cap in his meaty hands. He knew he shouldn't have stopped to talk to Sweet Katie at the fish market. Every time he talked to a pretty girl, his mind went completely blank. He should have come straightaway after getting the papers from the lamp on Baker Street.

Then suddenly it hit him. With a big smile on his dopey face, he pounded on the door, nearly breaking the brass knocker with his effort.

After a series of shuffling footsteps, the door swung open to reveal a greasy-looking manservant. The lank-haired butler didn't say a word, but stared at Chester with a pair of baleful eyes.

"I . . . I've come to see Mister Moriarty," Chester stammered.

"*Professor* Moriarty," the butler corrected. Then, after grimacing up at him, the butler stepped aside. Chester ducked his head beneath the door frame and entered the elegantly furnished apartment.

The place was dark, possessed by a gloom that no gaslight or kerosene lamp could penetrate. On the opposite wall from where Chester stood were countless trophies, the stuffed heads of ferocious beasts of one kind or another.

Chester stared at a huge rhinoceros head with a fang-like horn. The beady glass eyes looked so real that it was hard to believe the thing was actually dead. He shivered and took in the other creatures: the snarling mountain lion, several kinds of bear, and something else so strange and alien, with a tentacle mouth and large, insect-like eyes, that Chester couldn't tell what it was. The whole effect was terrifying, with each of the creatures forever frozen in an attitude of vicious attack or terror.

His eyes traveled down the rows of creepy-looking predators, finally settling on a shadowy figure that crouched beneath them. He couldn't quite determine what—or *who*—it was.

There was a hiss of steam. Then the shadow inched forward, rolling toward him on a pair of mechanical wheels. As it drew closer, Chester realized that it was Professor Moriarty. The sight of him couldn't help reminding Chester of an old spider, slowly emerging from its web.

"You were supposed to be here over two hours ago," the professor croaked.

Suddenly, Chester had no words. He stared at the man in

the chair as his mouth moved up and down with nothing coming out.

He was terrified.

"The photographs, you dolt. Did you bring the photographs or not?"

Chester felt his hand move automatically to his jacket pocket. He removed the small papers he'd taken from the gaslight and, with a shaking hand, passed them to the old gentleman. He'd long forgotten what it was that he'd wanted to say. Just being in the presence of Professor Moriarty had driven all thoughts from his head.

The professor gazed at the photos for several long moments, taking in the slightly blurred, sepia-toned images of Mrs. Hudson and Charlotte Pepper.

Then he glanced up at the hulking form of Chester Drummond and said drily, "On your way."

Chester hesitated. He'd suddenly remembered what he'd wanted to say to the professor, but was having difficulty summoning up the courage to say it.

"Well?" the professor growled.

"Sir, I . . . I was wondering . . ."

"Spit it out, man."

"Well . . . I wanted to . . . to know how much this job pays. I wasn't told how much I'd get when I said I'd do it," Chester finished awkwardly.

Professor Moriarty gave him a shrewd glance. "So what you mean to say is that you feel you deserve some kind of reward for your services, is that it?"

Chester beamed, happy that the professor understood what he was getting at.

"Yes, sir."

Professor Moriarty exchanged a knowing look with his butler. "I think that we can arrange something for you. Charles, please see to it that Mr. Drummond gets his payment."

And as Chester Drummond followed the butler into one of the side rooms, he began to wonder, even though he was severely lacking in the imagination department, if asking for such a thing from Professor Moriarty had been such a very good idea after all.

UPSIDE DOWN

Don't move, son," a kind voice said.

Griffin observed that the badge on the policeman's hat was extremely bright and must have been polished recently with tremendous attention, that it bore the number 271, that the man's hat size was approximately seven and three-eighths, and that the officer had cut himself shaving earlier that morning.

Then the next thing Griffin realized was that he was lying on his back, and there were pieces of broken carriage strewn all around him.

"Where am I?" Griffin asked.

"You're on Beacon Street," the policeman replied. "You were in a terrible accident, young man. And judging by the wreck and the size of the bullet holes in the wall of that cab, you're lucky to be alive."

Griffin tried to sit up, but in doing so felt waves of pain rush through his body. The policeman patted his shoulder gently. "Don't try to move just yet. You're going to be all right, but you've taken quite a walloping."

Griffin groaned and lay back. "It . . . it was a woman," he said.

The officer removed a small notebook. "Can you recall what she looked like? It might be tough, but anything that you can remember would be helpful."

Griffin shook his head, trying to clear it. "She was wearing goggles."

The officer nodded. "Hmm. Anything else?"

Griffin took a deep breath. Then, looking up at the officer, he said without stopping, "She was approximately five foot three in height and weighed one hundred and twenty-seven pounds. Her hair was an auburn color, shoulder length, and she had thirteen freckles across her nose. She wore goggles— aviator's goggles, I think—made by the ACME glass company of Long Island, New York. Beneath her glove on the third finger of her left hand was a lump; I assume it was some kind of ring . . ."

The policeman stared at Griffin with an incredulous expression as he rattled off the details.

". . . Her kid gloves were produced at a special tannery that services only a few shops in Bologna, Italy. I've seen that style twice before, and they're very expensive. The hat she wore had a large brim, was made of wool, and was also of foreign make. The bullet holes were fired from a gun made by Richard Gatling in 1861, but the gun was the smallest version I've ever seen. She also wore red lipstick and had a tiny scar on her forehead about one-quarter of an inch long, which looked to have been made by a sword point—a Scottish sword, I believe."

The policeman, who had been writing feverishly in his note-book up until this point, suddenly gave Griffin a skeptical look.

"Wait a minute. How could you know all this?"

Griffin shrugged slightly. "The scar had a particular squared-off shape, one that would match the tip of a Scottish Claymore. I also observed her stance in the carriage. Her feet were approximately ninety degrees apart and her knees were bent, very similar to a fencing stance. The Gatling gun I've seen once before in a museum, and I noticed the particular style of brass etching around the barrel of her weapon and that the signature *R. Gatling* was etched into its side. As far as the other details go, my mother's friend, Mrs. Newsom, has a pair of gloves that match the—"

The policeman held up a hand and chuckled. "All right, that's enough. I believe you." He grinned and shook his head in amazement. "If half of the officers I work with had your observational skills, we could rid the streets of crime for the next twenty years."

Griffin continued to give his detailed description to the officer. The policeman wrote down everything he said. And then, after Griffin had told him every single detail that he could remember, the officer thanked him and left, promising to do all that he could to catch the mysterious woman.

Griffin sat up and surveyed the wreckage.

It looked as though the carriage had exploded. Pieces of wood and carriage wheel spokes littered the streets. Griffin recognized one of the lanterns that had been attached to the cab lying on the fire escape of a building across the street, apparently thrown there from the collision. There was no sign of his or Rupert's luggage anywhere.

The more Griffin studied his surroundings, the more he realized that it was a miracle he had survived!

Then he was struck by sudden, panicky thoughts: Where was his uncle? And what about Toby?

As if in answer to his questions, Griffin suddenly felt something cold and wet snuffle the back of his head.

"Toby!" With a feeling of immense relief, Griffin turned and wrapped his arms around the happy pooch. The boy quickly studied the hound for any sign of injury and realized that the dog had somehow survived the crash without a scratch.

After giving him several hugs and pats, Griffin rose on shaky legs to continue observing his surroundings. He spotted his walking stick sticking out of a nearby apple barrel, and Toby trotted alongside him as he limped over to grab it. As much as he hated the thing and what it represented, he was glad to have it back. It wasn't just the blade hidden inside. Somehow, being without that stick—blade or no blade—made him feel more vulnerable to his enemy.

He wiped some apple pulp from the glittering silver knob with the edge of his coat and glanced around for the whereabouts of his uncle. There was no sign of Rupert anywhere! Griffin hoped that somehow his uncle had survived the terrible crash.

He glanced down at Toby, whose tail was wagging as he stared up at Griffin as if waiting to be told what to do next. Griffin knelt down beside his uncle's faithful dog and looked deep into his large, brown eyes.

"Toby, where's Rupert? Find Rupert!" Griffin held the hound's face between his hands, willing him to understand. "Rupert!"

Sherlock Holmes had called Toby "the best nose in London," and the claim was accurate. Toby was also a very intelligent animal, and he took off like a shot at the mention of his new master's name. Mr. Holmes had given the dog to Griffin's uncle Rupert as a gift. It had been offered as an apology for his once having been unable to help Rupert find his dog when he was a little boy.

Feeling hopeful, Griffin limped after the dog as fast as he could, following Toby across the street to a dilapidated-looking pub. Then, brushing aside his distaste for such places, Griffin pushed through the pair of swinging saloon doors and entered the darkened bar.

What he saw inside the dimly lit room made his heart catch in his throat.

A doctor was perched over the still form of his uncle Rupert. His uncle's face was crisscrossed with several cuts, and his arm was wrapped in a sling.

Toby whimpered and lay down beneath the table where his master had been placed. Griffin slowly approached the elderly doctor. He didn't want to believe what he was seeing.

"Is he . . ." Griffin choked, unable to voice the rest of the sentence.

But the doctor understood what he was about to say. He was a round-faced fellow with a bushy white beard, and was probably a jolly sort of person in another, happier setting. But because the situation he was currently in was so serious, he glanced up at Griffin and said quietly, "No. He's still with us. But he needs serious medical attention. I've sent for a carriage to take him to the hospital."

Griffin stared down at his uncle's unconscious face. Everything had happened so quickly! Just moments before they had been talking as they'd disembarked from the ship. He couldn't believe that things could turn so terribly wrong in such a short amount of time.

"Is he going to be okay? He looks very pale," Griffin said.

The doctor didn't meet his gaze. "I'm doing all that I can, son. He's lost a lot of blood, and his arm is sprained. I'm afraid if he doesn't wake up soon, he might remain in a coma. If we can get him to the hospital, they might be able to prevent it."

Griffin's stomach twisted. They were so close to his parents' home that he could have walked! He felt torn between worry over his parents' disappearance and his uncle's terrible state. All seemed misery and despair.

Without a second thought, Griffin did what came most natural to him at times like this. He prayed for mercy.

Please send help for my uncle, Lord, and help the ambulance drivers find their way quickly! And also, please be with my parents and keep them safe . . . wherever they are.

The second half of the prayer that he'd prayed so many times since leaving London almost came without thinking. But this time he was struck by how much he needed his parents. How Griffin wished they were with him now! What he wouldn't have given to have his father nearby, offering his strong support. Griffin knew that he would have had something encouraging to say, that he would have made everything feel under control.

But he had no idea where his parents were. Had Moriarty taken them someplace far away? Were they being tortured or, worse yet, had he done the unthinkable and taken their very lives?

His eyes filled with tears as he tried to imagine his father's gentle voice talking to him, calming him down.

And then something extraordinary happened. Griffin suddenly heard that same voice, but it wasn't inside his mind. It was really there! It was as if the very thing he longed to have most at that moment was actually happening.

Griffin spun around and stared, slack-jawed, at the lean man wearing a minister's collar. Griffin's eyes traveled over the familiar salty hair, the high cheekbones, and the same sad, blue eyes that he himself possessed.

"Griffin?" his father asked as he stared at his son, his eyes wide with surprise.

"Dad!" And without even pausing to ask how such an amazing thing was possible, Griffin rushed into his father's arms and hugged him as tightly as he could.

THE LADY RETURNS

The woman strode into the captain's quarters without knocking. She still wore her wide-brimmed hat and goggles but had changed her coat for a studded leather jerkin and trousers. Her long auburn hair tossed around her shoulders as she walked, and her lips were set in a grim expression.

The veil she'd worn when in the captain's quarters earlier had been a simple but effective way to observe her targeted prey and calculate how difficult it would be to "dispatch" them.

She'd been impressed by how quickly Griffin Sharpe had solved the little ruse about the lost telescope that she and the captain had come up with. But she'd also seen that the boy was naive and that his arrogant uncle was so oblivious to anyone but himself that it had been quite easy to capitalize upon their weaknesses. Neither of them had expected her surprise attack.

When she burst through the door to his quarters, the captain knew that it was she who was in command and not he. She was nothing like the meek and shallow tea sippers he entertained aboard his ship. This woman worked for the most dangerous man in London, and he knew that she was as deadly as she was beautiful.

"Miss Atrax," the captain said, smiling nervously and removing his cap. "It's an honor to see you again. I do hope that you'll make yourself comfort—"

"Sit!" the woman commanded, with a brisk Australian accent. The captain, who had been standing next to his desk, promptly sat down.

"I have completed my assignment. The boy and his uncle have been eliminated as planned. We must embark for London immediately."

"That was quick! Are you absolutely certain they were taken care of?" the captain asked.

"Nobody could have survived the wreckage," she said coldly.

The captain's smile collapsed. "Well, I . . . I'm afraid that it's quite impossible to travel to London right now. We're not scheduled to depart until tomorrow. None of the passengers are aboard. I'm sure that Mr. Moriarty would understand . . ."

The look that Miss Atrax gave him made the captain pause. Then, with her icy blue eyes locked on his own, the woman strode over to his desk. The way she walked couldn't help reminding the captain of some kind of predatory animal or insect. Her gait was slow, purposeful, and caused something inside of him, something deep and primitive, to feel a surge of panic as she drew closer.

She placed her gloved hands on the edge of his desk. Then she leaned over with her beautiful, pale face hovering just inches above his own.

"There is a certain spider in Australia commonly known as the funnel-web spider. Are you familiar with it?"

"I'm sorry?"

"The funnel-web spider," she repeated. "Are you familiar with it?"

The captain gulped and shook his head. "No."

"Pity," Miss Atrax said. Then she smiled, enjoying the man's obvious discomfort. "Allow me to enlighten you."

The captain watched as the woman tugged at the fingers of her left glove.

"You see, for many years, the male of the species was often referred to as the most dangerous spider on earth. But recently, scientists have discovered that the female of the species is just as deadly . . . if not more so."

Miss Atrax finished removing her brown kid glove. Then she lifted her left hand, turning it toward the captain so that he could get a better look at the ring that glittered on her third finger.

His eyes widened, noting the familiar shape. A diamond-encrusted spider crouched upon the band, its silver legs stretching almost to the lady's knuckle.

"Do you like it?" she purred.

The captain's mouth was suddenly very dry, and he felt unable to speak.

Miss Atrax continued while caressing the sculpture with the tip of her finger.

"The venom of this particular spider is extremely painful, and is nothing to be trifled with. You see, it is a hunter by nature and lays intricate traps for its intended prey."

She turned her attention from the ring back to the sweating captain. The captain saw her beautiful blue eyes crinkle at the edges, but he could tell that her smile never really touched their icy depths.

"People who live in Australia have to be very careful where they step, my dear captain. For if they should agitate the web of this very aggressive spider . . ." She paused to bare her teeth in a wolfish smile. "They tend to find themselves in a right bit of trouble. And oftentimes, it's much more than they can handle . . . if you get my meaning."

The captain licked his lips and nodded.

"My pretty ring here contains enough venom from that particular spider to kill a small elephant. So, if you please, I'd like to avoid using it on you and would humbly suggest that we embark for London immediately."

It was all the captain could do to keep from running as he strode from the room, heading directly to the quarters of his sleeping helmsman.

THE JOURNAL

Griffin pulled his thin legs up to his chin, trying to get comfortable in the chair by his uncle's hospital bed. The blanket that the nurse had provided him didn't bring much comfort, for he was much too anxious about his uncle's grave condition to sleep.

Griffin stared at his uncle's scruffy face, noting his receding hairline and his familiar bushy eyebrows. The moonlight illuminated his features, making them look even paler than they already were. Worry gnawed at Griffin's insides, and no matter how hard he tried, he found that he was having difficulty trusting that everything would turn out okay.

Please, God, let him wake up soon. It had been two days since the accident, and the doctors were growing more and more concerned.

He and his father were taking shifts by his uncle's bedside. Griffin was very thankful that he'd met his father at the tavern and had found out that both of his parents were okay and had not been kidnapped after all! His dad had been surprised to see the man he'd heard so much about from Griffin's mother, and had made sure that Rupert was given the best care that the hospital could supply.

After the joyful reunion with his parents, Griffin was relieved to find out that the sinister telegram must have been a hoax or a mistake. But the more he thought about it, the more Griffin realized he still wasn't sure about it. Something about the telegram hinted at a scheme, possibly something that Moriarty was behind.

Feeling worried, Griffin bit at his thumbnail while studying the bedside table next to his sleeping uncle. His eyes fell on his uncle's worn, brown derby. The lumpy hat sat next to Rupert's house key and his favorite leather notebook. It made Griffin feel a renewed sense of sadness as he stared at the familiar items. What if his uncle never woke up and used them again?

It was such a terrible thought that Griffin tried to push it from his mind, attempting to distract himself by counting things in the hospital room. Unfortunately for him, he had already counted the tiny flowers on the curtains (one thousand two hundred and twenty-three), the speckled tiles on the floor (eighty-six), and the tiniest stains near the baseboards (twelve) three times already and couldn't find many other things of interest in the room to count and ease his restless mind.

On an impulse, he reached over and took his uncle's notebook from the bedside table. Rupert had always been touchy about anyone looking inside of it, but Griffin was so desperate to relieve the long hours of waiting, he couldn't help himself. He hoped that under the circumstances, his uncle would have understood. Perhaps he would even find something written there that might be helpful to his uncle.

It was hard to see at first what was inscribed on the pages, for the distinctive brown ink his uncle used to write with was only slightly darker than the ivory paper. But as he studied the pale markings, Griffin realized what the pages contained.

His uncle's inventions!

A dazzling array of complex machinery, all carefully drawn with a fountain pen, sprawled over the notebook pages. Griffin felt that he had never in his life seen so many amazing ideas displayed at once!

Griffin marveled at his uncle's creativity. It seemed that there was no end to the things he planned to build. He slowly turned the pages, noting the name of each invention and the description and illustration beside each one.

The Snodgrass Sweeper. Next to the description, Griffin saw a sketch of a funnel-shaped device with a brush-driven propeller inside of it.

The Snodgrass Electronic Ear. A listening device held next to a man's head with curling wires extending for many yards in front of him. At the base of the wires, Griffin saw something that looked like the end of a doctor's stethoscope. He assumed that the invention was supposed to allow the listener to eavesdrop on conversations.

Could be useful, Griffin thought. *But not very polite.*

He turned the page.

The Snodgrass Foot Wing. Griffin tried to muffle a laugh when he saw the sketch. It was a mechanical wing attached to an old boot. Was it supposed to make someone fly or run really fast? In spite of his uncle's brilliance, Griffin felt that he might be prone to a couple of crackpot ideas once in a while.

He perused the rest of the journal, casually noting the many devices. Most were devoted to some aspect of self-defense or crime solving. But occasionally, there were sketches of things so unusual that Griffin had a hard time making sense of them.

He was about to return the journal to the bedside table when his eyes fell on the description of a truly remarkable device.

The Snodgrass Chrono-Teleporter. Griffin raised his eyebrows as he studied the illustration. He'd seen his uncle working on this device back on Baker Street, and Rupert had told him that it was shaping up to be the greatest invention he'd ever made. The mechanical drawing extended over several pages, detailing intricate clockworks and mathematical formulae.

But when he turned to the last detailed sketch, he had to smirk. All of this incredibly complicated machinery was contained in a very unlikely shell.

"Why, it's just a silly old teapot," he said.

"There's nothing silly about it, boy," croaked an irritated voice.

Griffin jumped at the sound. His eyes shot from the journal to the bed, and he felt the notebook slip from his hands, hitting the floor with a *thud* as he stared, unbelieving, at what he saw.

His uncle's eyes were open!

Happy tears blurred his vision as Griffin moved automatically to his uncle's bedside. Rupert, who was still very pale, stared up at him with a weak version of his usual scowl.

"It's not a teapot at all, boy," he growled. "It's a device made for traveling through time. Anyone with half a brain could've seen that."

But the outrageous claim didn't register with Griffin. All he could think about was the fact that God had heard his prayers and that his uncle Rupert was going to be okay. Relief flooded through him as he gave his uncle's hand a gentle squeeze. Then Griffin rushed back toward the door and called down the deserted hallway.

"Dad, come quick!" Griffin shouted. "Uncle Rupert is awake!"

HOMECOMING

The carriage ride from the hospital seemed to last an eternity to Griffin, and felt even longer for Rupert. Every jostle and bump elicited a cry of pain from the bruised and battered detective. The doctors had concluded that Rupert's arm had not been broken but was badly sprained and that his cracked ribs would be just fine in a matter of weeks. But Griffin's uncle was absolutely certain that the bumpy ride was bound to make the recovery last much longer.

While they traveled, Rupert scowled and spat at the slightest movement and used language that brought a blush to Griffin's cheeks. Hearing such fierce oaths, Griffin decided that it might be prudent to try to change the subject and get his uncle's mind off his injuries.

Griffin glanced over at his uncle and offered him a sympathetic smile. "Don't worry, Uncle. We'll be there soon," he said. "And when we get there, Dad said that Mother is sure to have a nice meal waiting for us."

"Not soon enough," Rupert growled, massaging his injured ribs.

Griffin sighed and looked out the window. *A fine pair of detectives we make*, he thought. With his limp and Rupert being down to one usable hand for a while, they looked more like the survivors of a battle than enquiry agents. But Griffin did notice that his encouraging words seemed to have a calming effect on his uncle. Rupert stopped swearing quite so much and suffered the rest of the drive in a pouty silence.

After about twenty minutes, the carriage turned up Beacon Street, and Griffin noticed the familiar landmarks that told him he was nearing his house.

There was the oak with fifteen branches; the fence with twelve posts, two knots, and seventeen wormholes. And next to that was the cobblestone path with one thousand three hundred and twenty-six stones . . .

He'd closely observed all his surroundings from the time he could count. He'd first noticed such details while toddling on walks with his parents as a three-year-old, surprising them as he made note of the distinguishing features of the objects around them. His parents had always been so proud of his observational skills, and in spite of his unique intelligence making him unpopular at school, he always knew that his parents loved him exactly the way he was.

Thinking of his parents, Griffin's mind drifted to the conversation he'd had with his father in the hospital shortly after Rupert had been taken there.

Griffin learned that his father had found him at the pub after the accident because he'd been making his usual rounds in the city, praying with people and visiting the sick. He told Griffin that he saw the wreckage and heard that there was a badly injured man inside the pub. When he'd caught sight of his son, he'd been so surprised that he'd nearly dropped the entire stew pot on the floor!

Now, many people would have thought it an amazing coincidence that they'd run into each other that day, but since neither Griffin nor his father believed in coincidences, they attributed it instead to an answer to prayer.

"The Lord works in mysterious ways," his father always said. And in Griffin's experience he'd found it to be true. After all, who in the world could have ever predicted that Griffin and his grumpy uncle would have become friends? That had to be heaven's work.

Griffin's dad had been further astounded when his son had told him about the false telegram that had said the Sharpes had been kidnapped, prompting Griffin and his uncle to travel immediately to Boston.

But there was still something that troubled him about the whole incident. If Nigel Moriarty was behind the attempt on his and his uncle's lives, why hadn't he just tried to get rid of them back in London? For the life of him, Griffin couldn't figure out why they'd been brought all the way to America just to be killed.

He mused over the problem as the cab turned down a side street and made its way toward the parsonage where his parents lived. They passed the First Methodist Church of Boston, Griffin's home away from home in the city. And upon rounding the familiar church with its tall steeple, Griffin felt a surge of excitement that temporarily drove the mystery from his mind.

He hadn't seen his mother in weeks, and it would be the first time that she and Rupert had spoken in many years. He could hardly wait to see her!

But then, after glancing over at his sour-faced uncle, Griffin realized that she might be in for a surprise. Her brother, Rupert, had lived with such bitterness toward his sister for so long, he wondered if his uncle could really find it in his heart to forgive her.

But Griffin couldn't help feeling optimistic about the progress his uncle had made. Since coming to live with him, Rupert had transformed into a much nicer person than the completely selfish, bitter man who had spent all of his waking hours obsessing over how to be a better detective than Sherlock Holmes. Certainly, some of his old habits remained, but Griffin knew that deep inside, his uncle was capable of much love.

And if there was one thing he knew for sure, it was that the power of love had the ability to change everything.

BROTHER AND SISTER

In a prison cell beneath the River Thames, where they had been held captive by Moriarty, Rupert had confided in Griffin that he'd been angry with Griffin's mother and hadn't spoken with her for many years. An incident had happened when they were children that had resulted in the loss of Rupert's dog, which had been his best friend in the whole world, and he had blamed Griffin's mother.

But after he'd poured out his heart, telling Griffin all that had happened, Rupert had been surprised to hear from his nephew how much his stepsister had missed him.

Griffin had proceeded to tell him about how his mother's eyes filled with tears whenever she mentioned her brother's name and that, even after so many years, she still called him by his affectionate, childhood nickname. She never understood why he refused to answer her letters, and the loss of her only brother had hurt her terribly.

After hearing these things, his uncle's heart had softened a bit. But years' worth of bitter feelings might be impossible to overcome.

Griffin looked at him now, noticing how the fading sunlight played on his uncle's scruffy, unshaven face and his graying hair. He didn't know exactly how old his uncle was, but if he had to guess, he would have said that he was probably in his late thirties. But with the deep, shadowed lines around his eyes, Griffin realized that Rupert could easily pass for fifteen years older.

The boy couldn't help but wonder if maybe his uncle's prematurely weathered appearance was because he'd been bitter for most of his life. Griffin knew that if it wasn't jealousy over Sherlock Holmes's success, Rupert was usually just as upset over the fact that he hadn't been recognized by the world as a great inventor.

It seemed that there was no end to his uncle's feelings that life hadn't treated him fairly. Which was a real pity, Griffin thought. Because even though his uncle couldn't see it, in Griffin's opinion he had much to be thankful for.

Now that the time to see his sister was at hand, Rupert seemed quiet and withdrawn. It was one thing to talk about forgiving someone when you were miles away and had little chance of seeing her, but it was quite another when you were moments from seeing her in person after not speaking for such a long time.

The carriage pulled to a stop outside the little stone cottage. Griffin's worry about his uncle shifted to excitement. He was home! Back home with his family, his own bed, his room with the view of the garden, and his books. All the things that he loved resided in this happy place, and now his uncle was there too!

The wheels had barely stopped moving when Griffin grabbed his walking stick and clambered out the door. His uncle wasn't far behind, moving slowly and muttering under his breath about the incompetence of the medical profession.

The door to the cottage swung open, and Toby came bounding out to greet them. Griffin's dad had taken him home from the hospital since pets were not allowed inside. The dog barked happily, rushing to Rupert as if he hadn't seen his master in months.

Rupert's face brightened at the sight of Toby, and he gently knelt down to caress the eager hound.

"Good boy," Rupert murmured. "That's a good boy."

Griffin was about to join his uncle in petting Toby when a familiar gasp made him stop. From somewhere behind him, he heard his mother's gentle voice. It sounded uncertain and worried as she called her brother by her affectionate, childhood nickname for him.

"Snoops?"

And then Griffin watched as his uncle rose from where he crouched, locking eyes with the sister he hadn't spoken to in twenty years. The two siblings stared at each other for a long time, their bodies casting long shadows in the fading sunlight. After a few moments the awkward silence grew unbearable to Griffin.

Say something, he urged silently.

Then Griffin's mother, whom he'd always known to be a reserved sort of person, let loose a loud shriek and ran toward Rupert with her arms extended.

Rupert's eyes widened as she grabbed him in a crushing embrace. To his credit, he didn't bellow with pain. But Griffin couldn't tell for sure if the tears in his eyes were because he'd been reunited with his sister or because of his injured ribs.

"Oh, Snoops, I'm sorry," his mother sobbed, her downcast eyes focused on his injured arm. "Are you hurt?"

Rupert looked at his sister. Then he lifted her chin gently and replied, "It's but a trifle. I'm all right, Cynthia."

And even though it sounded as though they were talking about his physical injury, Griffin knew that the forgiveness was meant to cover their unspoken quarrel too.

Then Griffin's mother turned to her son and wrapped him in a hug so tight that he felt almost smothered. Her scent, from a particular kind of lavender soap, which he'd known since he was a baby, brought him immense comfort.

"Oh, Griffin, I'm so glad you're home!" she said. And Griffin felt her warm tears dropping onto his head. His heart swelled with love for his mother, and he hugged her back as hard as he could.

All is right in the world, he thought. *Right here, right now.*

No matter what terrible things Professor Moriarty and his cousin were planning, they couldn't take away what he had. The love of his family. Maybe he and his uncle were a little beaten up and worse for the wear, but they were all together.

And there was nothing better than that.

QUESTIONS

Griffin had been lulled to sleep the previous night by the lilting sound of quiet conversation between his parents and his uncle. Hearing the peaceful drone of the adult voices and being able to snuggle beneath his own familiar bedcovers helped him sleep better than he had in ages.

But when he awoke the next morning, he was surprised to hear that they were still talking. After pausing to wash his face and comb his hair, he grabbed his walking stick and peered out into the living room.

His mother, father, and uncle were still sitting where they'd been the night before, and he could tell right away that they hadn't slept. They all wore the same clothes as the previous day and had that tired, disheveled look of people who had been up all night.

The morning sun cast long, mote-filled rays upon the three of them, illuminating them in a way that reminded Griffin of the stained glass pictures in his father's church. His heart swelled at the sight, for they were the people he loved best in the world.

They turned as he entered and offered him tired smiles.

"Sleep well?" Griffin's mother asked.

"Better than ever," Griffin replied happily. Then his curious gaze traveled over their concerned features. His mother indicated a pot of tea and a pile of warm teacakes on the coffee table.

"Sit down and have something to eat. They're your favorite. The lemon ones with vanilla frosting."

Griffin's mouth watered at the sight of his favorite dessert. But even as he picked up one of the wonderful pastries and took a huge bite, he couldn't get past the troubled look in his mother's eyes.

"Wait a minute; what is it? What's wrong?"

His mother and father exchanged worried glances. Then, realizing that it was nearly impossible to keep anything from their observant son, they sighed.

"Rupert has been telling us about some of the, er . . . 'adventures' you've been having over the summer," Griffin's father began.

Griffin glanced at his uncle but noticed that Rupert was staring out the window, consciously avoiding his gaze.

Griffin's father cleared his throat and continued. "We've all agreed that it might be better for you not to go back to London. This detective work you've been doing is much too dangerous."

Griffin's heart sank. He couldn't believe what he was hearing! Until this summer with Rupert, he'd never found a place to fit in and a way to use his gifts for something important. And now, after he'd finally found his calling, his parents wouldn't let him do it?

"Can't we talk this over?" Griffin asked.

He glanced again at his uncle, hoping to hear an argument

in his favor, but Rupert just stared silently at the battered bowler hat on his lap.

"Darling, we don't want you to get hurt again," his mother said gently. She glanced at the walking stick and frowned. "Thank the Lord you can still walk. But when I think about how close you came to . . . to . . ."

Her eyes welled up with tears. Griffin's father put his arm around her, stroking her shoulder. Griffin felt terrible to see his parents in such a state, but he felt equally miserable about the idea of giving up working with his uncle.

Griffin sat down next to his parents on the sofa and took his mother's hand.

"Mom, Professor Moriarty is the worst criminal in London, and his cousin, Nigel, is ruthless. He was the one who injured my leg and tried to kill me. If I can prove that he was behind this recent attack and help bring him to justice, then I can make sure that he doesn't hurt me again—or hurt the people I love."

Mrs. Sharpe stared back at her son, her lips compressed into a thin, worried line. Then Rupert finally spoke.

"Griffin, one of the main reasons we can't return to London together is because of the invention I've been working on, the one you saw in my journal and thought was just a teapot. The Snodgrass Chrono-Teleporter."

Griffin stared at his uncle. "I don't understand."

Rupert sighed and flicked an imaginary piece of dust from the edge of his bowler. "Like I told you at the hospital, it's something incredibly sophisticated . . . a time-traveling device. I've been working on it for many years with the help of a friend of mine, Herbert Wells."

"I'm not sure I understand what you mean by 'time travel,'"

Griffin stated. "Does that mean that it's some kind of portable timepiece? Like a strange-looking watch or something?"

Rupert chuckled. "No. It's a far more important discovery than that. With this device, a person can literally travel into the past or the future. At first, Herbert and I thought it was only theoretically possible. But the more we worked on it, the more real the project became."

Rupert stood from the chair and began pacing around the living room. "Herbert convinced me that if we could speed a person's atomic particles to match the speed of light, such a machine could actually work. It took years of research, but we finally managed to create one."

Griffin could hardly believe what he was hearing. *A time-traveling machine?* It sounded absolutely impossible. He looked over at his parents and could tell by their expressions that they thought the very same thing.

"We managed to send a sparrow into the future. The machine worked splendidly! But because we didn't know how to estimate how far into the past or the future we would send something each time we used the machine, I set to work to figure out a system to control it. This 'regulating gauge' has ended up being the hardest part to figure out. I was still stumped on how to solve it when you arrived in London."

He stopped pacing and gave Griffin a serious look. "The implications of what would happen if this machine fell into the wrong hands are too terrible to mention. What happened to us last time with Moriarty would be nothing compared to the terrible things he would do to get his hands on it. Herbert and I swore that we would keep the machine secret. But now I fear that my friend Herbert might have let the cat out of the bag. Look here."

Rupert retrieved a copy of the previous day's newspaper from the coffee table and handed it to his nephew. The headline read, "Noted British Author H. G. Wells Missing. Authorities Fear Foul Play."

The article went on to detail the disappearance of the famous writer. Scotland Yard didn't have a single clue. It was as if he'd vanished completely. But that couldn't be. There had to be someone or something behind it. After reading the article twice, a horrible thought suddenly occurred to Griffin. Glancing up from the newspaper, he fixed his uncle with a frightened stare.

"Oh no," he said. "Why couldn't I see it before? It's so obvious!"

Rupert looked perplexed. "What is?"

Now it was Griffin's turn to get up and pace around the room. "I should have realized it sooner. Moriarty arranged the telegram to get us out of our apartment so he could steal your machine!"

Rupert's already pale complexion faded to a chalky white. Griffin's mind raced, putting the pieces together. The more he thought about his theory, the more sense it made. Moriarty had arranged to get them to America so he could steal Rupert's time machine. And while they were abroad, he could arrange to have them killed. It would be far more difficult to trace the incident back to him when they were so far from London.

There was a long silence. Mr. and Mrs. Sharpe stared at their son, looking frightened. Then Griffin's mother spoke to Rupert. "If this machine is as dangerous as you say, are there innocent lives at stake?"

Rupert nodded, still looking stunned. "If Moriarty gets his

hands on the machine, he could use his knowledge of past or future events to change the world. I'm confident that he would use it for nefarious purposes," he said.

He wrung his hands anxiously. "I did take precautions before we left London to make sure that the machine was carefully hidden. I'd have brought it with me, but I didn't want to risk it getting broken. But experience has taught me that Moriarty is very resourceful. I had no idea that he was planning on stealing it!"

Mrs. Sharpe paused before replying. Then she asked, "And do you honestly think that, if he has stolen it, you can't stop Moriarty without Griffin's help?"

Griffin watched as his uncle was forced into admitting something that he hadn't been able to admit before. It would have been very easy for Griffin's uncle to take the position that he always had, that he was someone completely capable of handling everything himself and that the only reason he wasn't the greatest living detective on earth was because somehow fate and circumstances had kept it from him.

But since his and Griffin's last encounter with Moriarty, changes had been working within him. And even if those changes were slow in being realized, they had affected the way Rupert looked at himself and the world.

There was an evident struggle as he forced himself to utter words that were painful for him, that in the past he never would have heard himself say.

Rupert took a deep breath and, shaking his head in resignation, said, "No. I don't believe I could do it without him."

BACK AT THE BOSTON DOCKS

The eyes and ears of the Moriartys were everywhere, stretching from London and watching and listening in all corners of the globe. Regular reports came into the professor's many secret headquarters, and the information was passed through the shadows and alleys, traveling along twisting paths and strands until the news he needed reached the heart of his web.

And such ears and eyes were also present at the docks of Boston Harbor. In a shadowy corner near a weathered-looking sail repair shop, a pair of Professor Moriarty's ears belonged to a blind beggar named Silas, and a pair of his eyes to the beggar's monkey, Peanuts.

As the beggar turned the handle on his rusted calliope, he wasn't listening to the piping music. His task was to identify the comings and goings of everyone on the docks, and because of the absence of sight, he'd developed his hearing to an uncanny ability.

So when Silas Grunge heard the *tap-tap-tap* of Griffin's cane, his eyebrows raised in recognition. For Silas knew the exact noise that that particular cane made, having heard it on many other occasions back in London. Its hidden blade had cost him his sight, and he would never forget the particular ringing its tip made as it clinked against the cobblestones, each one sending shudders through his bony frame.

If there had been any doubt that it was the two people whom he'd been instructed to listen for, Peanuts confirmed it for him. The monkey, trained as a pickpocket, slid its dexterous paw into Griffin Sharpe's jacket as he walked up the gangplank to the ship and withdrew as evidence the pocket watch given to him by Frederick Dent.

Even with his legendary gifts of observation, Griffin Sharpe was completely unaware of the loss of the watch, his attention turned instead to maintaining control of the frenzied Toby, who wanted more than anything else to attack the chattering monkey.

Peanuts gave the timepiece to his master. And after running his gnarled fingers over the surface and recognizing exactly what it was, blind Silas Grunge pocketed the watch and with unexpected speed dashed down a nearby alley to the back door of a nearby telegraph office.

Within moments, the message "BOY AND SNODGRASS ALIVE stop ATRAX PLAN FAILURE stop RETURNING TO LONDON" blazed across electric wires, traveling the long cables to London like vibrations sent down a spider's web.

And Silas knew that the old, gray spider that waited on the other side would not be pleased by the news that these two juicy flies had escaped his clutches.

BAKER STREET

The long journey home was an anxious one for Griffin and Rupert. All either of them could think about was getting back to the apartment as soon as possible.

They paid the hansom cabbie twice his normal fare, and the cab flew down the London streets at a reckless pace. They arrived at 221 Baker Street in record time, and Griffin and his uncle jumped out of the carriage and hurried up the front steps to their apartment. In spite of the urgency, with Griffin's expert gaze he couldn't help but notice subtle changes to the apartment that once belonged to Sherlock Holmes. For one thing, the dingy mat that had always been outside the door had been replaced by a newer, cleaner-looking one. And second, the window that faced Baker Street had been decorated with new curtains, delicate lace that looked as if it were made from spiders' webs.

These things registered in the split second it took for Rupert to remove his key and throw open the door to their dwelling, and, although noted by Griffin's inquisitive mind, he didn't really have the time to give it much thought.

They strode into the foyer.

"I'll get the lights," said Rupert.

But before he took another step, a mysterious man-sized shape hobbled forward out of the darkness.

A thief! Griffin thought. Seeing no other way to defend himself, he raised his cane as if to strike.

"Master Griffin, Mr. Snodgrass, welcome home," came a flat, mechanical voice. As the shape drew nearer, Griffin recognized Watts, his uncle's mechanical manservant.

"Hello, Watts," Griffin said, feeling relieved. Under usual circumstances, he would have been overjoyed to see the marvelous invention and to engage him in a lively discussion, but he was too worried at the moment to make conversation.

He hurried past the robot, following his uncle into the inventing room. *Please let it still be there*, Griffin prayed. He remembered the exact spot where his uncle had been working on the device and hoped beyond hope that he would see the Chrono-Teleporter lying there, undisturbed.

Rupert turned on the gas lamps, illuminating his cluttered inventing area. After Griffin had had his accident, his uncle had made an attempt to clean up the room. But old habits die hard, and soon the chaotic clutter of invention had once more possessed the crowded workspace.

"I'll be right back," Rupert said. "Please stay here," he added. And before Griffin could say a word, his uncle had hurried back out through the front door.

Griffin scanned the countless piles of bolts, bulbs, wires, gears, cogs, and clock faces. Something looked wrong. Although at first glance everything seemed undisturbed, for some reason he felt certain that everything he saw was slightly rearranged, like someone had been there while they were gone and had rummaged through his uncle's things.

Griffin wondered where his uncle was. He assumed that he had gone to wherever his secret hiding spot for the Chrono-Teleporter was.

Suddenly, he heard his uncle burst back into the room. And to Griffin's immense relief, it wasn't but a moment later when he heard him cry, "All's well!"

Griffin wheeled around to see his uncle marching toward him with an ordinary brown teapot in his upraised hands. Griffin recognized it immediately as the Chrono-Teleporter sketched in his uncle's journal.

"Where . . . ?" Griffin started, but fell silent. He could tell that Rupert didn't want to discuss the location of his secret hiding spot.

"I'm sorry, nephew, but that must remain a secret. I haven't told another living soul about the location, and, as you can see, it has ensured the safety of the machine."

Griffin tried not to feel hurt because his uncle didn't trust him with the location. His naturally inquisitive mind didn't like secrets. But he respected his uncle's privacy and understood his reason for not wanting to share the information.

Rupert grinned and set the device on the fireplace mantel. "Safe and sound, eh, my boy? We had nothing to worry about after all."

Griffin nodded and let out a long sigh. The amount of time he'd spent worrying had taken a toll on him. He suddenly felt completely exhausted, as though he could crawl upstairs to his bed and sleep for a week!

A sudden knock on the door made them both jump. After

exchanging quick, puzzled looks, Rupert lifted one of the many futuristic weapons he kept mounted on the wall and slowly approached the door. Griffin followed, wishing he still had his Stinger, but the pistol had vanished along with his luggage during the carriage incident back in Boston.

"Who's there?" Rupert barked, standing just behind the door.

"Your new neighbor," came the lilting reply. Griffin and his uncle exchanged puzzled looks for a second time, and with a shrug, Rupert lowered his futuristic-looking rifle and carefully opened the door.

"Hello. I am your new neighbor," said a young woman wearing a silken dress of bright blue and white gloves that went all the way up to her elbows.

Griffin's cheeks colored the moment he saw her, for she was very pretty. Rupert was so stunned that he just stood for several moments with his jaw working up and down and no sound coming out.

"You must be the great detectives Rupert Snodgrass and Griffin Sharpe. How delightful to meet you both," the lady chirped.

And without even waiting to be asked inside, she entered the apartment. They watched as the beautiful young woman set a basket down on the kitchen table and began unpacking a delicious-looking tea.

"Er . . . excuse me, Miss . . . ah . . . ," Rupert said, finding his voice at last.

"Pepper," she replied. "Charlotte Pepper. The newest resident of Mr. Sherlock Holmes's famous address."

She handed Rupert a jar of lemon curd. "Open this, please."

Rupert stared at it for a moment, then automatically did as he was asked. Handing the jar back to her, he said awkwardly, "Mrs. Pepper, if you don't mind my asking—"

"Miss."

"Beg your pardon?" Rupert asked.

Charlotte Pepper took the opened jar from Rupert and placed it on a tray next to a dish of clotted cream.

"*Miss* Pepper. I'm not married," she said briskly.

Rupert's face turned bright red, and he cleared his throat. "Yes, yes, of course, I didn't mean to . . ."

"To what, *Mister* Snodgrass?" she asked playfully. "To insult me? Well, I assure you that it is no insult. I am twenty-four years of age and not married, and I don't intend to be so for many years to come. I am quite capable of looking after myself and see the whole institution as distracting from my work."

Griffin noticed that his uncle's hands were fidgeting, nervously straightening his tie. He had never seen him act this strangely before.

"And, er, what kind of work is it that you do, if you don't mind my asking?" Rupert said, his voice cracking a little.

Without hesitation she replied, "Like you and your young nephew, I am also a detective."

Griffin noticed that her words seemed to have a powerful effect on his uncle. Rupert stared at his neighbor with a look that could only be described as total and complete adoration.

Griffin couldn't help chuckling at his uncle's odd behavior. When he'd first come to live with him, Rupert had been completely obsessed with despising his neighbor, Sherlock Holmes, seeing him as a threat to his very existence. But this time, a second detective at Baker Street evoked the opposite response.

Charlotte Pepper must be an exceptional person, of that there could be no doubt. For within five minutes, she'd completely transformed Griffin's perpetually scowling uncle into a grinning puppy dog.

Which made Griffin suddenly think of something important. With a start, he turned to his uncle.

"Uncle! We forgot Toby!"

"Hmmm?" Rupert said. He was intently watching Miss Pepper unpack the delicious tea and seemed unable to register anything else.

Griffin pulled at his uncle's sleeve. "Toby, Uncle. We were in such a hurry that we forgot to get him from the ship's kennel!"

Rupert suddenly snapped back into focus.

"Toby!" He smacked his palm onto his forehead. Then, turning to Miss Pepper, he said in a ridiculously formal voice, "I'm terribly sorry, my dear Miss Pepper, but we shan't be able to join you in what looks to be quite an excellent tea." He indicated the beautiful array of freshly baked scones, jam, cream, and sandwiches with a bow and flourish of his hand.

Griffin's stomach rumbled, and he couldn't help feeling a little upset that they had to interrupt what was bound to be a magnificent meal.

If Charlotte Pepper was disconcerted by this, she didn't show it. She continued setting out the tea, adding some elegant silver spoons to the place settings.

"Well then, be off if you have to, but return as soon as you can. The scones came out of the oven just five minutes ago, and the sooner you return the more delicious they will taste. I'll be here when you get back."

Griffin hesitated. Up until that moment, he'd been intrigued by this forceful person who had shown up bearing gifts and assuming a level of comfort and intimacy that was usually reserved for old acquaintances. But as he thought about all of his uncle's secret inventions, especially the Chrono-Teleporter, he wasn't sure it was a good idea to leave a stranger in the house while they were gone.

To his surprise, his uncle didn't seem to share his reservations. Rupert placed his battered bowler back on his head and smiled broadly.

"Of course, my dear, of course. We shan't be gone long, and should you need any assistance at all, Watts will take care of you."

Rupert called down the hallway to his metal servant. "Watts, I want you to see to Miss Pepper's every need. See to it that she's made absolutely comfortable."

Hearing the mention of his name, the metal man clanked into the kitchen and raised a hand of welcome to Miss Pepper. For the first time, the girl seemed at a disadvantage, gaping openly at the brass man with his sculpted metal mustache and bowler.

"Mr. Snodgrass!" she finally exclaimed, clasping her hands together in delight. "I had heard that you were a remarkable inventor, but I had no idea you were capable of such genius!"

Rupert flushed with pleasure and, to Griffin's horror, let out a very unusual, high-pitched giggle. Then, before he had a chance to voice his concerns, Rupert wheeled from where he stood and, taking his nephew's arm, said in a very jolly sort of voice, "Come along, nephew. We have a pup to rescue and a lovely lady that we don't want to keep waiting."

"Um, Uncle, aren't you forgetting something?" Griffin said

quietly. He nodded his head in the direction of the parlor, where the time machine was sitting on the fireplace mantel.

Rupert started. Griffin could tell that he'd been so distracted by the lovely Miss Pepper that he'd almost forgotten.

"Oh yes. Of course." Rupert bowed to Miss Pepper as he quickly marched back into the parlor. He returned a few seconds later, looking relaxed.

Griffin couldn't help noticing that he hadn't gone back through the front door, to the spot where he'd hidden it before.

"Is everything . . . er . . . okay?" Griffin asked.

"Fine, my boy." Then Rupert leaned close to Griffin's ear and whispered, "I doubt we have anything to fear from our guest. But to be safe, I tucked it away out of sight."

And the next thing he knew, Griffin was shoved out the door and was bounding down the steps, trying to keep pace with an uncle whom he thought he knew, but who was now acting like a completely different person.

THE SPIDER'S WEB

iss Jane Atrax was hanging upside down. Her long auburn tresses dangled beneath her, her hat and goggles were gone, and she was bound neck to ankle in iron gray cables. Her mouth was gagged, but her eyes spoke loudly enough. They were wide with an expression that not many could produce in such a formidable woman. Just days before, she had been the predatory spider, but she was now the fly. And she was terrified.

"Ah, Miss Atrax. So good to see you again!"

Professor Moriarty wheeled into the immense cavern, followed by his cousin, Nigel. The torch-lit cave cast eerie shadows on both men's faces, making them look, if possible, even more sinister than they already were. Miss Atrax struggled in her bonds, powerless against the heavy cables that held her fast. Nigel Moriarty chuckled as he watched her panicked writhing, evidently enjoying her discomfort.

"Now, now, my dear, you mustn't overexert yourself. The gentleman who was here before you tried to do the same, but then found that he had used so much of his energy trying to break free that he had none left to fight his adversary."

The old man gestured with long, delicate fingers to a discarded cap lying near a rocky wall. "Poor Mr. Drummond. He came to a very messy end."

Miss Atrax wondered at the professor's use of the word *adversary*. She didn't know what diabolical plan the Moriartys had in store for her, but if she had been afraid before, she was doubly so now.

"Now then, we should get to business." The professor smacked his lips and rubbed his hands together. He nodded at Nigel, who approached Miss Atrax and removed the cloth that covered her mouth.

"I . . . I'm sorry, sir. I don't know how the boy and his uncle survived the crash. Nobody should have survived such an explosion. I shot over two hundred rounds into the carriage and used a bomb to finish them off. It's impossible!" the woman said, her voice rising in panic.

Professor Moriarty clucked his tongue. "Ah, but you see, my dear woman, the fact is that they *did* survive, which was *improbable*, but not, as you say, *impossible*."

Miss Atrax bit her lip. She watched as Nigel Moriarty approached a metal box that was wired into the cavern wall. He whistled softly as he opened the box and revealed a switch inside.

"I'm an old-fashioned gentleman, Miss Atrax. The kind of person who doesn't enter into a bargain lightly. When I hired your Black Widow Society, I expected each of your talented ladies to perform their duties as specified in our agreement," Professor Moriarty said. "You didn't eliminate Mr. Snodgrass and his nephew; therefore, you must pay the price of your failure. Now I can only hope that your counterparts can succeed where you failed."

Nigel Moriarty threw the switch. With a loud groan, the floor beneath the place where Miss Atrax dangled began to vibrate. She watched as two heavy metal doors slid slowly apart, revealing a deep pit beneath her. What she saw below her turned her insides to jelly, and if it hadn't been for the fact that she was hanging upside down, she would have run away screaming.

It was an elegant thing, in the way other deadly things, such as scorpions or black widow spiders, are elegant. It was as if, in their design, nature sent warning signs that said, "I'm beautiful, but stay away! Beware! Don't touch!"

The horrible thing moved on several heavy, mechanical legs. Its sleek, curved body was painted glossy black with curling red pinstripes that ran artfully up its torso, ending at a transparent dome. Inside the dome was something like an electronic brain, all flashing lights and strange, clicking machinery. It had claws, powerful claws, that were made to crack bones and squeeze the life out of its intended victim. They snapped ominously at the dangling woman as the cable she was tied to lowered her down, down, down to its waiting grip.

Miss Atrax knew beyond a shadow of doubt that she was no match for the thing. And as the cable finally eased her down to the floor of the pit, she did something that she hadn't done since she was very young.

She let out a long, terrified scream. And as it turned out, it was the last sound she ever made.

TEA FOR THREE

It had taken over two hours for Griffin and his uncle to locate Toby at the docks. Apparently, there had been a mistake with the shipping clerk, and the poor hound had accidentally been shuffled off to some fishing boat along with two tons of especially foul-smelling fish.

But what made the situation more exhausting was Uncle Rupert's constant babbling about Miss Pepper. He kept saying things like, "Yes, my boy, that Miss Pepper is a deucedly fine woman," or "Charming sort of person, Miss Pepper," or "One can see that Miss Pepper is a remarkable lady. She's obviously the possessor of a fine mind. I do believe that in Miss Pepper, we finally have a neighbor worth having!" and "We should ask Mrs. Hudson about the possibility of gathering the tenants of Baker Street for dinner, especially Miss Pepper. It would be the neighborly thing to do."

"Miss Pepper . . . Miss Pepper . . . Miss Pepper."

The two had barely met and his uncle was completely smitten! Rupert was acting so incredibly different from the sourpuss his nephew had come to know that the boy was at a total loss for what to say in response to his ceaseless chatter.

When they finally found Toby, the dog was so relieved to see his familiar masters that he nearly broke the bars of his cage in his eagerness to get out. The best nose in London had not fared well surrounded by stinking fish, and the poor pooch howled piteously as Rupert fumbled with his key ring in an effort to get to the one that opened the padlock. When the door finally swung open, Griffin was knocked completely off his feet and was smothered with more wet doggy kisses than he could successfully fend off.

After rescuing Toby, it took Griffin and Rupert quite some time to flag down a cab, for it was nearly nine o'clock by the time they'd gotten the dog back. And as fate would have it, that cab turned out to be much slower and less reliable than the one that had gotten them to Baker Street earlier that day.

Griffin was starving, and the ride was long. But Rupert was even more agitated than Griffin was, often yelling at the cabbie to hurry and pounding on the ceiling of the cab to make his point. Evidently, for Rupert, the thought of returning and finding that Miss Pepper had given up waiting for their return was too much for him to bear.

They finally arrived back at Baker Street at a quarter past ten, and Griffin felt certain that the wonderful tea that Miss Pepper had arranged earlier would be gone. As he and his uncle sadly marched up the stairs to the darkened apartment, he was reminded by an unpleasant rumbling in his stomach that he hadn't eaten in several hours.

And those scones had looked delicious, he thought miserably.

As the door to the apartment swung open, Watts made his

usual greeting, the brass man's electric eyes glowing in the darkness and his mechanical voice stating its usual, "Welcome home." After his uncle lit the gas lamps, Griffin was surprised to find a note from Charlotte attached to a basket left on the kitchen table.

Waited as long as I could but assumed that you ran into some trouble. I added a jar of pickles and some cold beef to go with the scones. I'm terribly sorry that I am unable to join you. Perhaps we could have tea another time in the near future?
—C.P.

At first Rupert was crestfallen. But then he whistled in appreciation when he pulled a jar of his favorite Branston pickles from Miss Pepper's basket. Griffin's mouth watered with renewed vigor at the promise of the delicious-looking meal. After all the delicacies were unpacked, Griffin noticed that the teapot that Charlotte Pepper had brought with her earlier wasn't among the basket of goodies.

Oh well, he thought. *The tea is sure to be cold, anyway. We can have Watts brew us some more.*

He turned to his uncle and said, "It was certainly nice of *Miss Pepper* to leave this for us, wasn't it?" Then, unable to resist the urge to tease his uncle more, he added, "That *Miss Pepper* is a deucedly fine woman, don't you think?"

At first Rupert smiled back at him with such warmth that Griffin hardly recognized him. But then, realizing that his nephew was teasing him, Rupert suddenly went redfaced and snorted with offended dignity.

"You really like her, don't you?" Griffin asked, his eyes twinkling.

"Nonsense," Rupert replied gruffly. Then, after preparing two plates of scones and roast beef, he added, "I'm just being neighborly, that's all. She's a nice woman and very . . . generous."

But Griffin had to stifle a laugh, knowing that his uncle was trying to hide his obvious feelings. And although Griffin felt happy that Rupert had met someone who had struck him with such immediate feelings of affection, there was a tiny part of him that was bothered by the encounter. There was something about Miss Pepper that was familiar and that he didn't like. Something troubling that he couldn't put his finger on . . .

And it wasn't until much later that night, after all the dishes had been cleared away and all the sweets and savories eaten, long after he and his uncle had retired to bed, that he realized that what troubled him wasn't something he "couldn't put a finger on." It was something that Miss Charlotte Pepper had put her finger *in*.

A BUMP IN THE NIGHT

Her ring! Griffin's eyes snapped open. It had just occurred to him why he'd felt uneasy with Miss Pepper. As he was falling asleep, the image of Charlotte Pepper's gloved hand unpacking the tea popped into his mind. He remembered seeing a large lump beneath the glove on the third finger of her left hand, the same exact place he'd seen such a ring-shaped lump before. It was strange that she'd said she wasn't married, and yet she wore a ring like a married woman would have.

And not only that, but the woman in the carriage had had a ring just like it.

He could recall in vivid detail the shooter's left hand as it held the trigger of the Gatling gun. And as he compared the images of her hand and Miss Pepper's in his photographic memory, the sizes and shapes of the ring-shaped lumps were identical.

Suddenly, a loud bump from downstairs startled him. He stared around wildly in his darkened room.

What was that?

It couldn't be his uncle. Rupert was notorious for getting to bed on time, often quoting the American inventor Benjamin Franklin's favorite line, "Early to bed and early to rise makes a man healthy, wealthy, and wise."

And besides that, something Griffin sensed told him an intruder was in the house. It was difficult to pinpoint exactly how he knew it, but there was a definite *wrongness* about the sound, and it sent chills up his spine. Griffin's hand automatically reached to his bedside table, where, since his last near-fatal adventure, he'd always kept his Stinger. But as his fingers brushed the empty surface of the table, he was reminded again of his lost luggage and the bag that had contained his unique weapon.

"Drat," he murmured. His thoughts flicked to the wall of futuristic weapons downstairs, and he desperately wished that he'd thought to bring one of them, any of them, upstairs when he went to bed.

Griffin heard another rustling sound downstairs and then the sound of the front door closing. With his heart thumping wildly, he pulled aside his bedclothes and retrieved his dressing gown. Then, gripping his walking stick, he crept out of his room as quietly as he could, trying very hard to avoid stepping on any creaky floorboards.

Because of his keen observation skills, Griffin knew which spots on his bedroom floor made the most noise. As he tiptoed slowly toward his door, navigating in the near-pitch-black darkness, he pictured the room vividly in his mind.

Five steps to the right, now a big step over the floorboards bedside the wardrobe, shuffle to the left, then another big step forward . . .

Navigating around the creaky spots, he made his way soundlessly to the stairway and cautiously descended the stairs. He held his breath, aware of no sound but his pulse thumping in his ears.

As Griffin reached the bottom stair, he carefully slid the sword from inside his cane. It was the first time he'd unsheathed it with the intention to defend himself, and as much as he hated the thing, it seemed his only choice for protection.

With one hand using the cane scabbard for support and the other gripping the three feet of razor-sharp steel, Griffin rounded the corner and walked toward the living room. He felt cold and couldn't tell if it was because the temperature in the house had changed, or he was afraid.

He squinted in the darkness, trying to discern any unusual shapes or movements that would alert him to the intruder's presence. Then, just as he walked into the living room, a voice sounded from behind him.

Griffin was so startled that he wheeled around and swung the sword at the source of the voice. There was a tremendous *CLANG!* and a shower of sparks as the weapon glanced off something hard and metallic. Then two figures leapt from the shadows and rushed past him. He swung his sword wildly at the smaller of the two shadows and heard a sharp cry. But the wound wasn't enough to stop the intruders as they leapt out of the window and fled the scene.

Moriarty's henchmen! he thought, imagining the woman who had shot at him in Boston. He rushed to the window but was too late to catch sight of the thieves. All he could hear was a clatter of retreating footsteps on the cobblestone streets.

When he turned back to face the room, he saw the bluish

glow of Watts's incandescent eyes staring back at him in the darkness, and Griffin thought that if there was any way a machine could look at him reproachfully, this would be it.

"Would Master Griffin require anything?" Watts's flat, mechanical voice said. Griffin noticed that Watts's metal derby had a large dent in it, apparently made when Griffin had wildly swung his sword.

Feeling embarrassed, Griffin dropped his sword arm to his side. "Sorry, Watts," Griffin said. "I didn't know it was you."

The gas lamps flared to life all around him. Rupert stood there, looking wild-eyed and disheveled, his thinning hair pointing up in all directions. Griffin supposed that the sound of his sword hitting Watts's metal head must have startled him awake.

"What the deuce is going on?" he shouted.

But before Griffin could answer him, his uncle's eyes automatically flicked to the opened window. With the lights on, Griffin could see for the first time just how disordered the room looked. Someone had definitely been there. "A prowler?" Griffin said, half to himself.

But then Griffin saw something that made his heart freeze. As he walked slowly over to the fireplace mantel, he focused on a new object that hadn't been there before.

He reached up and took down Charlotte Pepper's elegant teapot, the same one that she'd brought to tea earlier. And there, attached to the teapot handle and tied with red string, was a prettily folded note.

It took a moment for Rupert to register what had happened, but when he did, his eyes grew wide and his skin paled. He gestured shakily for Griffin to hand him the note. Griffin felt sick. Someone had clearly broken into their home and stolen the time machine right out from under their noses.

After opening the letter, he and his nephew stared at the beautiful handwriting, unable to believe what they were reading.

Messrs. Snodgrass and Sharpe,

I hope you'll accept in trade for your remarkable teapot this one of my own. I do appreciate you inviting me in and leaving me to care for the premises in your absence this evening.

The location of the time machine has eluded me for several weeks. Until tonight, I feared that you had hidden it so well that I could never hope to find it.

However, when you hurried back into the parlor before you left, I felt that perhaps what I sought was within reach. I had just deduced its location when you returned, and had to put off taking it until you were asleep.

Please do not hold anything against dear Mrs. Hudson for helping me break into your apartment. She was compelled to do so, by means that I am not free to discuss. I have left the key she gave me on the kitchen table.

I shan't be needing it any longer.

Mr. Wells was helpful in describing the invention's function, but he failed to mention the charming container in which it was housed. I must offer my compliments on using something so decidedly British to contain the greatest invention of the modern age.

I must insist that for your own safety you do not try to follow me. You are up against forces that even the great Sherlock Holmes would find daunting, if not impossible, to prevail against. In a few hours the world as you know it will have completely changed. Professor Moriarty plans on rectifying the years of thwarted plans and failed capers that have plagued him so.

He insists that a new history begins tonight and that the hands of the ancient clock will be turned and the very stones themselves will be rearranged.

Oh, and a second word of warning. Very few have met Miss Atrax in battle and lived to tell the tale . . . Your escape will be duly noted by the entire Sisterhood of the Black Widow.

And now I must be off. TIME is, indeed, of the essence.

With warm regards,
Charlotte Pepper

Rupert finished reading the note aloud and let it slip from his fingers. Griffin, feeling weak, eased himself down onto one of his uncle's threadbare chairs. It was terrible, too terrible to even think about. With the time machine at their disposal, Professor Moriarty and Nigel could wreak havoc. By changing the events of the past, they could effect for themselves a future where justice couldn't prevail.

"We've lost," Rupert mumbled. "We'll never find her. She's too good . . . She took me in and fooled me completely."

Griffin's heart nearly broke when he heard the hurt and despair in his uncle's voice. His uncle had barely gotten to know Charlotte Pepper, but it was evident that he'd fallen quite hard for her. To have such a beautiful young woman suddenly seem so interested in him must have been an unexpected and exciting twist in Rupert's life.

Griffin had to admit, his first impression of Miss Pepper was hard to shake. She seemed so nice! But he was reminded strongly of the story of Lucifer, an "angel of light" who, against all appearances, was capable of great evil.

Griffin's dad had often told him the old saying "One shouldn't judge a book by its cover," and in this case it was certainly true.

Griffin picked up the note and read it a second time. As he scanned the lines, his eyes suddenly widened in surprise. There was something there that he hadn't seen before—a clue! A clue that told him that even when it seemed all was lost, there was still hope of tracking down the stolen device!

But even as he discovered this information, Griffin was also acutely aware of the danger they would be walking into. If what he thought was right, then the words Charlotte had written about Sherlock Holmes thinking twice before pursuing her were probably true.

Griffin rose from his chair and, taking his uncle gently by the arm, said, "Uncle, I think I know where Miss Pepper went."

Rupert Snodgrass gazed down at his precocious nephew uncomprehendingly.

"What?"

"Miss Pepper," Griffin repeated. "I think I know where she's taken the time machine."

Rupert suddenly snapped to attention, his eyes focused on his nephew with a desperate, hopeful expression. "Where?" he demanded.

Griffin paused before replying, "I'd rather not say just yet. But if it's where I think it is, then I'm pretty sure we're going to need assistance." He gazed up at his uncle with his sad, blue eyes. "And there's only one person in all the world that I think we can trust to help us."

THE RETURN

Nigel Moriarty marched down the stone corridor, his eyes alight with knowledge and hidden purpose. His lips were twisted into a bitter scowl, and the right leg of his trousers was shredded. Beneath the pant leg, bloodstained bandages, hastily wrapped, could be seen peeping through.

In spite of his tattered appearance, the professor's cousin seemed filled with a vigor that defied his middle years. For he held something underneath his arm that was and was not from the world in which he lived. And the thing that he'd found while on his unusual journey would change his and everyone else's lives forever.

He didn't hesitate before entering his cousin's private chambers. His was a rare privilege, the ability to enter the inner sanctum unannounced. This hidden lair was the most secret of the professor's holdings. Unlike the warehouse apartment, it was a location so private that only the highest ranking and most dangerous of Moriarty's henchmen were allowed to know about it.

Nigel turned the lion-headed knob and opened the heavy door. Then he stepped inside the lavishly apportioned room.

The room was lit by the bright glow of electric light, a rare luxury. Furnishings of the finest quality were arranged around a Persian rug, a carpet that Nigel knew came from a Turkish prince. Nigel hid his jealousy over his cousin's wealth behind a carefully constructed mask of indifference. He couldn't let on that he planned to make them his own by any means necessary.

"So, you have returned," croaked a voice. Nigel turned and saw the familiar, spidery shape of his cousin's steam-driven wheelchair emerge from the shadows. "Because the world around us appears to be quite unchanged, I deduce that you were unable to properly affect the past."

Nigel shook his head. "The blasted machine is completely unpredictable. That idiot Snodgrass didn't create a way to pinpoint where and when a person can travel. All it's got on it is a switch that says 'Past,' 'Present,' and 'Future.' The only thing that can be safely relied on is, once a trip is embarked upon, the machine will return to the point of departure. That's it. Otherwise, I would have never gotten back."

The professor studied his cousin's battered leg. "And you had a bit of trouble, I take it?"

"Tyrannosaurus rex. Barely escaped with my life."

"And what have you got under your arm?" the professor said, eyeing the small package.

"After numerous attempts, I decided that I wasn't getting anywhere. So I made a leap into the future and found this."

He removed the wrapped package from under his arm and handed it to his cousin. The professor studied the unusual bag for a moment, noting the strange, florid colors that decorated its surface and the unique material of which it was made.

"Some kind of synthetic material. A chemical compound woven together by scientific means. Hmmm." He examined it more closely, studying the words *The Book Loft* printed on its surface.

Nigel had a hard time containing his impatience. He wanted his cousin to get on with it. The bag wasn't important; what was inside it was.

After what seemed an eternity, the professor finally reached inside the bag and pulled out a hardback book. When he saw the title, his eyes grew wide.

The Complete Adventures of Sherlock Holmes by Sir Arthur Conan Doyle.

He cracked open the book and scanned the table of contents. "A collection of that fool doctor's magazine articles. Nigel, I asked you to come back with historical documents, not sensational stories. The only consolation I have is that in the future, James Watson has been relegated to obscurity by a usurper. Someone who has apparently taken credit for his writing . . . this Conan Doyle chap. Humph."

But before Nigel Moriarty had a chance to respond, his cousin spotted what had made Nigel buy the book. Listed among the various adventures was a collection of stories titled *The Casebook of Sherlock Holmes.*

"Ah. Now here indeed is something of interest." He turned the pages to the back of the book and began to skim the text. After a brief moment his sunken eyes flicked to his smug cousin. "I see now why you brought this to me. Well done, Nigel."

In that section of the book were future cases that Professor Moriarty hadn't been a part of yet. They were plans and capers that he had been formulating as recently as that morning, but he could see now that all of them had been thwarted by Sherlock Holmes.

The book, of course, made no mention of Professor Moriarty by name. After the accident at the Reichenbach Falls, the one that had robbed him of his ability to walk, everyone had believed him dead. This was, of course, perfect for the professor, who could now control his vast criminal empire without suspicion of being linked to any of the crimes.

"The arrogant fool," the professor said, referring to Holmes as he turned the pages and read. "It seems that no matter what I do, he thwarts me. However, this book does tell us something. It tells us exactly where Sherlock Holmes will be. Each of these cases has yet to happen, and if we plan accordingly, we can determine what time and place to spring a trap."

He pointed at one of the cases listed among the future events, one called "The Lion's Mane."

"See here, Nigel. This account gives us the precise location of Sherlock Holmes's new residence, along with where he will be when the events of this particular case unfold. Hmmm." Moriarty rubbed a gnarled forefinger along his massive temple. After a long moment, he spoke.

"Take this." The professor removed from his waistcoat pocket a glittering silver ring. Nigel recognized the beautifully crafted spider as once having belonged to Miss Atrax.

Professor Moriarty continued, "I was planning on trying the particular venom contained in that ring on Miss Pepper, but, considering the circumstances, we shall postpone. It's time we gave Mr. Holmes's illustrious career a surprising twist."

Nigel smiled, his curled, gray mustache tilting upward in an evil grin.

For him, the worst part of traveling to the future was finding out that his name was completely without mention in any of the history books. He'd always thought himself a great man, and finding that he had been given no credit for his misdeeds had wounded his pride. Only his cousin was known, mentioned in popular culture as Sherlock Holmes's greatest adversary. In the future, the name Nigel Moriarty was forgotten.

But now that he possessed this knowledge, he was going to make sure that he changed that. After tomorrow, when he paid a visit to Mr. Sherlock Holmes, things would most certainly be different.

He would be *remembered*.

THE BEEKEEPER

As Griffin disembarked from the carriage, he was greeted by a stiff ocean breeze. He looked about him, taking in the majesty of the Sussex coast. The towering white cliffs contrasted beautifully with the cobalt sea. Gulls squawked overhead, and the thatched roofs of whitewashed cottages dotted the landscape in the distance.

Even the carriage horses seemed to appreciate the place, for they stamped their hooves and shook their manes as if anxious to break free of the wagon and run down the sandy beach.

Griffin couldn't deny the air of peace and relaxation, and for the first time since leaving the London apartment, he smiled. The stress and worry over the time machine's whereabouts vanished as he leaned on his walking stick and gazed at the wonderful countryside. He could definitely see why Sherlock Holmes had chosen this location for his retirement. The Sussex Downs were gorgeous.

And part of the peace he felt was the certainty that now that they'd arrived, they would have the help they needed. Somehow, in spite of how grim everything looked, he felt certain that with Sherlock Holmes's help and advice, everything would turn out okay.

A grumpy voice interrupted his thoughts.

"Not much to look at, is it?" Rupert groused as he stepped from the carriage.

"You don't think so?" Griffin asked, genuinely surprised.

Rupert scowled at the pleasant cottages and picket fences. "Country people. Always meddling in each other's affairs. A bunch of busybodies, if you ask me."

Ever since the incident with Miss Pepper, Griffin's uncle's sudden cheery outlook on life had been replaced by his usual disgruntled attitude. And as they walked along the steep path that led to Sherlock Holmes's new address, with Rupert complaining at every step, Griffin was struck by his uncle's unique ability to see the dark side of everything. It was as if he and his uncle were two sides of a magnet, positive and negative poles that were somehow, impossibly, drawn together.

To distract his mind from the slew of complaints and negative comments, Griffin focused instead on counting the paving stones on the charming pathway (five hundred and six), the number of lilacs in the trees (fifty-seven), the butterflies he spotted fluttering by the wildflowers (three), and swarms of honeybees (three hundred and sixty-six). And while counting these things, he consciously chose to ignore the one hundred and thirty-five times that his uncle used the word *stupid*.

Trying hard to remember to be patient, Griffin limped toward the beautiful pine door of Sherlock Holmes's quaint little cottage and knocked gently with the tip of his cane.

There was no answer.

I wonder if he's out, Griffin thought. He knocked again to be sure. And this time, after waiting for a full minute and hearing nothing, he interrupted his uncle's rant.

"Um, excuse me, Uncle. I wonder if we should check in the back and see if he's there. Do you think it would be all right?"

". . . idiots. Er, what did you say?" Rupert asked, confused by his nephew's interruption.

"I was wondering if we should check the backyard. Perhaps Mr. Holmes is there but couldn't hear us knocking," Griffin repeated.

Rupert paused and scratched his stubbly beard. After a long moment he replied slowly, "No, I think we should just leave. If he is in there, he obviously doesn't want to be disturbed."

Griffin couldn't help noticing the relieved look on his uncle's face as he turned on his heel to go.

"Don't you think we should at least check?" Griffin said.

Rupert stiffened. He glared at Griffin, hating that he couldn't come up with a good enough excuse to avoid seeking help from Sherlock Holmes. Griffin could tell that Rupert was annoyed, but the boy quietly stood his ground. He knew, in spite of his uncle's reluctance to work with Sherlock Holmes, that every second lost at this point was precious.

So he felt an immense sense of relief when Rupert gave a resigned growl and pushed past him, making for the little white gate at the side of the house.

As they went through the swinging gate and down the path along the side of the cottage, the first thing Griffin noticed was that the drone of bees grew increasingly louder. He puzzled over this, but when they rounded the back of the cottage, he discovered why the hum had reached such a high level.

Large white boxes were stacked on top of each other, each

one surrounded by swarms of the buzzing insects, filling the enormous backyard as far as the eye could see.

"Hives," Griffin murmured excitedly, recognizing the bees' dwellings. He'd forgotten that Holmes had mentioned he planned on becoming a beekeeper as part of his retirement.

Griffin smiled, thinking about all the fresh honey that the bees were making. He imagined that out here, where there was so much wild clover, the honey they made would taste absolutely delicious.

He was just about to mention this to his uncle, when something out of the corner of his eye caught his attention. He had to look twice to be sure, but it appeared that there was something sticking out from behind one of the rows of white boxes. Something in the grass that looked suspiciously like . . .

A human foot?

An inexplicable feeling of dread suddenly washed over him. He wondered if he was seeing things. He hoped he was wrong, that maybe he was just seeing a twisted root or a discarded piece of wood. But something inside him knew that probably wasn't the case.

With equal parts curiosity and dread propelling him forward, Griffin inched step-by-step toward the strange and horrible sight.

"Griffin! What are you doing?"

He was dimly aware of his uncle's call. His mind was focused on what he was looking at. *Just a few steps more and I'll know for sure.*

He was so intent on finding out who or what was behind the boxes that he could barely hear his uncle's cries. Then suddenly he felt something large and heavy clap down over his head.

He felt his uncle's big hand on his shoulder, wheeling him around. Then, startled, he saw Rupert's angry face staring at him through a veil of thin, web-like netting.

"Don't be stupid, boy. Keep yourself covered!" Then he adjusted the beekeeper's helmet that he'd placed on Griffin's head so that no bees could penetrate the netting.

"Of all the senseless things to do . . . Why do you think bee-keepers wear these things? For a fashion statement?"

Griffin was about to reply when he noticed his uncle's eyes glance over at the thing in the tall grass that was now only a few yards away.

"What the deuce?"

Griffin could see through his beekeeper's veil that his uncle had gone very pale.

"Is that . . . what I think it is?" he asked.

"I think so," Griffin replied. "But there's only one way to know for sure."

They shared a meaningful glance. Then Griffin and Rupert carefully walked over to the row of white boxes. As they drew closer, Griffin saw that what he'd spotted in the grass was indeed a foot.

But far worse was finding out *whose* foot it was.

There, stretched back between the rows of white boxes, was a motionless figure in a beekeeper's uniform, lying on the ground.

Griffin knew at once that the person was dead. There could be no doubt about it. But even though he knew it, he still couldn't resist running over and, after removing the figure's bulky glove, checking the body's pale wrist for a pulse.

There was none.

And although there was a tiny part inside of Griffin that had feared that this would be what they would find, he wasn't prepared for the awful sight.

It was Sherlock Holmes.

The great detective's helmet had been knocked aside, and a thin stream of smoke still curled upward from his beekeeper's firebox. Perhaps it was the smoke, but the bees seemed to be avoiding the area around his body. Impossible though it seemed, to Griffin it was almost as if the tiny insects were showing respect by not stinging the one who had cared for them so.

His hands shook as he turned to look at his uncle. Rupert stared back, equally stunned.

"What should we do?" Griffin whispered.

Rupert didn't say anything at first. The look he had on his face as he stared down at Sherlock Holmes, his longtime rival, was something Griffin would never forget in the years to come. It was a look filled with sadness and genuine loss, as if his world would never be the same again.

Griffin knew that the relationship Rupert had with Sherlock Holmes was somewhat akin to that of a younger and an older brother. While he'd lived next door, his uncle had been consumed with jealousy, rivalry, and bitterness at living in the great detective's shadow. But now that he was truly gone, it was as if Rupert had lost something that had defined who he was.

For who was Rupert Snodgrass without Sherlock Holmes? In many ways, the great detective had always been his measuring stick. Having Holmes living next door had pushed Rupert to become the best inventor he could possibly be, if only to try to find a way to beat the detective at his own game.

Holmes had also shown true remorse over not having been

able to help Rupert find his dog when he had been just a boy. By way of apology, Holmes had given him Toby as a replacement. The dog had been an amazing gift, something that Rupert had never expected.

But now, as Rupert stared down at Sherlock Holmes's pale, unmoving form, all the jealous feelings that he'd harbored over the years were gone. All he could see before him was the loss of a truly great man, one for whom the world would never find an equal.

Sherlock Holmes was the greatest detective who ever lived.

"We need to get him inside," Rupert whispered. Griffin could tell that his uncle was trying to contain some powerful emotions.

Griffin nodded dumbly. But then, as he was stooping to pick up the detective's legs, Griffin suddenly stopped. His uncle stared at him.

"What is it?" he asked.

Griffin didn't answer. He walked over and knelt down next to Sherlock Holmes's right hand. It was balled into a tight fist.

Griffin pulled at the long fingers. It took some effort to get them to release what they were holding. But after some persistence, they gave way. Griffin exhaled slowly, staring down at the large and glittering thing that lay displayed on Holmes's outstretched palm.

It was a spider-shaped ring.

And he knew immediately that it was the exact size and shape of the ring that belonged to both Charlotte Pepper and the woman who had shot at them from the carriage.

Griffin stared at the intricate design of the spider, noticing the sparkling diamonds that encrusted its beautifully crafted body. He was just about to pick up the ring when his uncle's hand shot out, catching him by the wrist.

"Careful," Rupert warned. "There's something about that ring I don't like."

Griffin glanced up at his uncle and nodded. It was indeed a wicked-looking thing. Rupert removed a pair of long tweezers from his vest pocket and lifted the ring from Holmes's hand. As it was taken away, Griffin let out a gasp.

"Uncle, look at his palm."

They stared down at the inflamed area where the ring had been nestled a moment before. They could clearly see two small puncture marks in the center of Holmes's hand.

Griffin inspected the ring that his uncle held more closely. After studying it for a moment, he noticed two tiny, retractable barbs embedded in its jeweled thorax.

"I think that's what did it," Griffin said.

Rupert grimaced. "Poisonous." He glanced back at the ring he held with the tweezers. "I wonder *who* did it."

Griffin didn't tell his uncle about his suspicions. For the moment he decided that it would be better to wait. He didn't know which one of the two women was the culprit, but when he thought about Charlotte Pepper's note and how she'd bragged about being in the service of Professor Moriarty, it certainly looked as if she might be the one to blame.

"I suppose we should get him inside now," Griffin reminded his uncle.

On the count of three, they lifted. Griffin tried not to think about what he was doing, willing himself to put one foot painfully in front of the other. Walking without the support of his stick was difficult, but he hardly noticed the discomfort. All he could think of was how the world would take the news when they found out that the greatest detective who ever lived was gone.

They made their way through the back door of the cottage and laid him on the living room sofa. After looking around, Rupert was relieved to see that a bit of modern technology had been installed in the cottage and used the wooden, hand-cranked wall telephone to call for help.

While his uncle used the telephone, Griffin stared down at the still form of Sherlock Holmes. A tear rolled down his cheek as he gazed at his sad, angular face. Holmes would no longer prowl the streets, keeping his keen watch over the innocents who trusted him. No longer would criminals fear the shadows, knowing that a human bloodhound would find every bit of evidence they left behind and bring them to justice.

Sherlock Holmes was dead.

And the worst part for Griffin was knowing that the great detective had been murdered.

THE FUNERAL

On the day of Sherlock Holmes's funeral, it didn't rain. The sun shone down upon the grassy cemetery of Christ Church Newgate, and the birds chirped. But the sun also caused long shadows to fall, and, in Griffin's mind, the shadows that stretched across London were darker than ever before.

As he limped along with the long procession of policemen and well-wishers, following the pipers as they played the traditional dirge, "Flowers of the Forest," Griffin heard snatches of conversation from the crowd. Most people said things like, "Mr. Holmes was a great man," or "What'll we do without him?" but he also thought he caught snatches of darker talk, a word or two whispered between disreputable types expressing their joy over the great detective's demise.

"The old professor got 'im in the end, didn't he, Jim?"

"'At's right. The old hound went a-sniffing where his long nose didn't belong."

Because the crowd of mourners was so thick, Griffin couldn't see who had said these things, but the comments made him feel sick to his stomach. He realized that for as many law-abiding citizens who were devastated by the loss of their protector, there were just as many criminals who had been longing for this day to come.

The procession stopped near Holmes's final resting place. Griffin was glad to find himself situated near a stump, for he was too short to see over the towering mass of adults. Climbing upon it, he had an excellent view of the tall monument that had been placed there by the grateful city. And although he was a fair distance from the huge stone, he could still make out the bold inscription engraved on the polished marble.

SHERLOCK HOLMES
THE WORLD'S GREATEST DETECTIVE

After reading these words, he couldn't help glancing over at his uncle. Rupert was dressed, like Griffin, in his Sunday best. His uncle's black frock coat gleamed and stood in sharp contrast to his battered brown bowler. Rupert had been determined to wear the hat in spite of Griffin's insistence that it looked so bad as to seem disrespectful. But he didn't press the point. Just getting his uncle within a mile of a church was a major feat in and of itself.

Rupert was scowling at the inscription on the monument. And Griffin knew his uncle well enough to know that seeing the words *The World's Greatest Detective* on Holmes's tomb bothered him, almost as if they were a written insult directed at him. Rupert had always thought his investigative methods superior to Holmes's. But now it seemed that this memorial would forever cement in people's minds that Holmes truly was the greatest detective who ever lived, and not he.

Griffin sighed and turned his attention back to the funeral. Would his uncle ever get over himself? Why did it seem that everything revolved around him and his pride? But then, Griffin realized, the temptation to feel important in other people's eyes often had to do with a deep need to be loved. He reminded himself to try to feel more compassion for his uncle, rather than to judge him too harshly. After all, standing in judgment of his uncle was just another way of being prideful himself.

They were both too far away to hear the minister's sermon. But Griffin could see Dr. Watson and his wife standing next to the preacher, looking sorrowful. Until that moment he hadn't considered how Dr. Watson would be feeling. The good doctor had lost his best friend and colleague. What must it be like to lose such a close friend and to know that there were no more wonderful adventures to write about? And worse still, to know that with Holmes out of the way, Moriarty could rule London unopposed?

Griffin certainly didn't think that he and Rupert were as threatening to the Moriartys' criminal empire as Sherlock Holmes had been. But the very fact that the professor and Nigel had tried to get rid of them in Boston told him that they weren't insignificant. And now that Holmes was gone, Griffin and his uncle were the only ones who stood in the way of the evil men and their nefarious schemes.

Griffin gripped his ebony walking stick, staring down at Nigel Moriarty's familiar initials engraved on the cane's top. Then he looked out at the sea of Londoners gathered together, most with heads bowed and hats clutched to their chests. Many of the ladies were wiping their eyes, and there were children in attendance too.

He felt a surge of empathy as he spotted one child, a little girl of about five or six, clutching her mother's skirts. He could imagine what she must be feeling, seeing her parents in such distress. She happened to glance at Griffin at the same time he was looking at her.

Who will protect you now? he wondered.

But even as the thought popped into his head, he already knew the answer. It was his job now.

THE OLD CLOCK

tonehenge? You can't be serious!" Rupert said.

Griffin placed a pair of clean socks in his small pack. "It's the only place that makes sense," he replied.

He had hoped to get confirmation from Sherlock Holmes on this point and to find out if he knew anything about how well guarded Moriarty's secret hideout would be. But with the great detective gone, it had fallen upon him to arrive at his own deductions.

"And how exactly did you determine that there's a secret lair hidden beneath Stonehenge?" Rupert asked. "I don't see any evidence that points to such an outlandish conclusion."

Griffin took Miss Pepper's note from his pocket and handed it to his uncle.

"Miss Pepper changes her writing style in the middle of her letter. If you read the first part of the note, it sounds like she's giving us some insight into her thinking. She's obviously very proud of her accomplishment and wants to tell us so. Take a look," Griffin said.

Rupert scanned the note, reading the parts where Charlotte

informed them of how she deduced the location of the time machine and how easily she managed to break into their apartment. He glanced up at Griffin, scowling.

"An arrogant woman. Obviously lacking in social graces."

Griffin tried not to laugh. To hear his uncle criticizing someone else for being arrogant and rude was pretty funny.

"She does seem confident," he agreed. "But if you look closely, you'll see that there is a line or two that stands out as something other than just bragging. See here," Griffin said, indicating the end of the note. "It's like she decided to be poetic all of a sudden." He read the lines aloud to his uncle: " 'A new history begins tonight . . . the hands of the ancient clock will be turned and the very stones themselves will be rearranged.' "

"It's like I said. The woman possesses an overinflated ego," said Rupert.

"Oh, but I don't think so," Griffin said excitedly. "Why would she say 'the hands of the ancient clock'? What could she possibly be referring to?"

Rupert shoved his hands into his worn trouser pockets. "I don't know," he said grumpily. "Perhaps she's talking about time itself. After all, she does possess the time machine."

"That's what I thought at first," Griffin admitted. "But then I wondered, why wouldn't she just say 'the hands of time will be turned'? Or something simple like that? To me, it sounds like she's hiding something." He indicated the next part of the note. "And listen to this part: 'The very stones themselves will be rearranged.' "

He glanced up at his uncle, his eyes dancing with excitement. "I don't know if you know this, but there are some people who believe Stonehenge was an ancient clock, a way for early inhabitants of Britain to keep track of time and the seasons."

The scowl disappeared from Rupert's face as he considered Griffin's words. He inspected the note closely for a moment, then turned back to his nephew.

"It might be a coincidence," he said.

"It might," Griffin replied. "But I have a hunch—"

"Oh, bother hunches and all that nonsense!" Rupert exclaimed. "I want facts, boy, facts!" He slapped his fingers across Charlotte's note.

Griffin tired hard to keep his annoyance in check. It might not be fact, but his hunch was the best lead they had.

"But, Uncle, do we really have any other leads? Doesn't it seem like we should at least try this theory and see if it works?"

With a sigh, Rupert finally agreed. "Very well. We don't have anything else, and a good detective always eliminates all possibilities before jumping to conclusions."

Griffin watched as his uncle walked over to his display of inventive weaponry. He proceeded to remove two guns: a rifle with a strange-looking scope mounted upon it, and a small pistol.

"Is that the Stinger 2?" Griffin asked, filled with excitement. He had missed his little gun. But as his uncle drew closer and handed him the weapon, he saw that it was something else entirely.

"No. But the Snodgrass Scorpion is nothing to be trifled with," his uncle said brightly.

"What does it do?" asked Griffin.

"Aha!" his uncle replied. "That is the best part. Are you ready for this?"

Griffin smiled and nodded, feeling hopeful.

Rupert waited, allowing the mystery and excitement to build. Then, with a grand gesture, he waved his hand and pronounced, "This incredible device does absolutely . . . NOTHING!"

Griffin stared. Was he serious? He glanced back down at the pistol, unable to hide his disappointment. They were about to head into what could possibly be the most dangerous place in Britain and he would be carrying a *fake* gun?

"I can tell what you're thinking, my boy, but don't jump to any conclusions yet," Rupert said, offering him a rare smile. "When I say 'nothing,' I mean exactly that. The weapon you're holding shoots an anti-matter ray. It literally removes physical objects from existence, transporting them to another place entirely!"

What? Griffin stared at his uncle with awe. Was he serious?

"Allow me to demonstrate," Rupert said. He pointed the small pistol at a dented oilcan on the floor. There was a bright flash, so blinding that Griffin saw green spots dancing in front of his eyes. When his vision cleared, he looked at the spot where the can had been resting just moments before.

It was gone without a trace.

Griffin shook his head, unable to process what had happened.

"Where did it go?" he asked.

Rupert grinned and shrugged. "I have no idea," he replied. "It could be anywhere. It has dematerialized and is probably somewhere halfway across the world by now."

"Amazing!" Griffin cheered. He was about to congratulate his uncle on yet another of his ingenious devices when something suddenly fell from the ceiling and clouted his uncle soundly upon his head.

"Ow!" Snodgrass shot his hand to his forehead and rubbed it vigorously. "What the deuce?"

Griffin tried not to laugh as he observed the oilcan that clanked to the ground just a few paces from where it had been before. Apparently, the Snodgrass Scorpion had its limitations.

"That usually doesn't happen," he said while massaging the small bump on his head.

"Are you okay, Uncle?" Griffin asked.

"I'm fine," Rupert said gruffly. He straightened his coat and tie and tried to look dignified. Then he handed the small weapon to Griffin. "Use it with caution. As you can see, the results can be, ah, unpredictable."

Griffin gazed down at the small gun, inspecting its beautifully etched barrel and walnut handle. In spite of the mishap, he could tell that it was a truly remarkable invention. And, most importantly to Griffin, it wasn't designed to kill anyone. He knew that sometimes force was necessary when dealing with evil men like Moriarty, but he didn't have to like it.

"Thank you, Uncle," Griffin said. "It truly is an extraordinary weapon. I'll be careful with it."

Rupert grunted in satisfaction. Then, after digging around in a cabinet, he produced a holster for Griffin to carry the Scorpion, as well as a long strap that allowed Rupert to carry his own special rifle on his back. Intrigued, Griffin wanted to know all about the futuristic-looking rifle, but his uncle merely replied with a cryptic arch of his eyebrow, "It's too complicated to explain at present. However, I can assure you that this weapon has a few surprises that our enemies will never expect." And even though Griffin continued to prod him a little, his uncle wouldn't say any more about it.

They quickly finished packing. Rupert glanced at his elegant pocket watch, the same one given to him by Frederick Dent after the Westminster Clock case, and said, "We must hurry if we want to catch the train to Wiltshire. It's almost three o'clock!" Griffin lamented the loss of his own watch, having discovered its absence on the boat trip back to London. For being as observant as he was, it was rare when an object he cared about went missing. It hadn't taken him long to deduce that the monkey must have taken it back in Boston Harbor. He determined then and there that if he ever had the chance, he would make sure to track it down when he returned to America.

They made it to Charring Cross station with five minutes to spare. It was hard for Griffin to keep up with his uncle because of his hurt leg, but the conductor held the train back when he saw them approaching so that there was enough time for Griffin to get aboard.

As the conductor made his ticketing rounds and the train began to pull away from the station, Griffin's hand moved to the small holster hidden beneath his jacket. He was feeling a growing sense of panic. It had been almost two days since Charlotte Pepper had disappeared with the teapot. He knew that after obtaining the time machine, the Moriartys would have wasted no time using it to execute their plans. He had no idea what they were planning to do, but he knew that with something that powerful, it would be terrible. He only hoped the teapot was as unpredictable and difficult to control as his uncle claimed, since it might buy them a bit of time while their enemies tried to figure it out.

But Griffin didn't have to wait very long before finding out exactly what the Moriartys were up to. For, as the train pulled away from the station, something outside the window caught his eye. And as he stared at it, unable to comprehend what he was seeing, his uncle Rupert noticed his gaze and looked out of the window too.

And for the first time, both of them were rendered speechless by what they saw.

CHANGES

It was due to the fact that Griffin possessed such extraordinary observational skills that he spotted the lettering on an important-looking building as the train sped out of the station. The sign read Moriarty Savings and Loan.

"How is that possible?" Griffin said, perplexed. "Do the Moriartys own a bank?"

Rupert shook his head. "He's been to the past," he muttered. "And he's already changed it."

A thrill of fear washed over Griffin.

"What do you mean?" Griffin asked. He suddenly felt very small and helpless. His uncle gazed back at him with a flat expression.

"That sign wasn't there before," he confessed slowly. "They have obviously wasted no time using the machine. Until recently, that sign read Bank of England."

Griffin's mind reeled. The letters on the side of the bank had appeared to be quite old, but the name of the bank had changed. If the Moriartys had seized control of the banking system, what else could they do? The implications were staggering!

He'd barely contemplated the question when his eyes fell on a newspaper tucked between the seat cushions. The headline read, "Nigel Moriarty to Be Named Prime Minister."

"Uncle, look!"

Rupert snatched the paper from his nephew and read the terrible headline.

Griffin felt a rising wave of panic. It was all happening so fast! History was changing in front of their eyes and at a pace that neither of them could believe. But then, with a start, Griffin realized that it all made sense. The Moriartys had all the time in the world. They could travel to the past at their leisure, and the changes would be instantaneous in the present.

"Unless we get the Chrono-Teleporter back and stop them, we haven't any hope at all," Rupert said.

Griffin's observational skills suddenly kicked into overdrive. He took stock of everything in his surroundings, staring out the train window as they passed through London, wondering all the time what terrible changes had happened from the present he used to know. The worst thing about it was that there was no way for him to tell what had changed and what had always been there.

And that's when a sudden thought occurred to him.

"Uncle?"

"Yes?"

"How can you know if everything has changed? I mean, if our entire lives have been affected by changing the past, then we shouldn't know any differently. Everything would seem completely normal."

"Ah, that." Rupert glanced at his nephew, noting his troubled look. He smiled and said, "Good observation, my boy. But that's precisely why I invented the Snodgrass Paradox Recorder."

"What's that?" Griffin asked.

"A microscopic machine. Roll up your sleeve."

Feeling confused, Griffin did as his uncle asked. Rupert reached into one of his leather satchels and removed a doctor's syringe. Griffin stared at it apprehensively. He'd never liked shots!

"What are you going to do?" Griffin asked.

Rupert didn't reply. Griffin nervously watched as he squirted a bit of green fluid from the syringe. Then, before Griffin had a chance to prepare himself, Rupert swiftly injected its contents into his arm.

"OW!" shouted Griffin.

"There," said Rupert, removing the needle. "Nothing to worry about. The Paradox Recorder will travel through your bloodstream and attach itself to your cornea. Everything will be fine."

"My eye!" Griffin exclaimed.

"Yes, your eye," Rupert said matter-of-factly. "I already installed one in mine. Don't worry, my boy. Your vision will remain completely intact. But from now on, you'll notice that whenever something has changed from the present that you and I are originally from, a light glow will appear around it. Not only that, but you'll be able to accurately recall your own present, no matter what tampering is done to your personal timeline."

Rupert smiled proudly. "It is definitely one of the more ingenious things I have created." Then he added, "Sometimes, I'm so brilliant I even surprise myself."

The thought of one of his uncle's inventions microscopically attaching itself to his eye made Griffin feel nervous. At least Rupert could have asked him first! However, since it was already done, Griffin had no choice but to trust his uncle and hope that everything would work as described.

While rubbing his arm, he turned his gaze out the train window and back to the London streets, looking for any signs of the glow his uncle described.

The first thing he noticed was that there was an absence of constables patrolling the streets. Then he gasped. For, just as Rupert had predicted, Griffin could suddenly see that the areas of pavement where the policemen normally stood now emitted a pale white glow.

Amazed, he looked around for other signs that the past had been tampered with. Griffin noticed the countless broken shop windows on every corner. Streets that had once been filled with happy London families now swarmed with displaced children, poor and bedraggled, without any parents to be seen. The orphans seemed to be present on every corner, selling matches or begging alms.

And all of these things glowed with a strange, pale light.

Moriarty had certainly been busy!

Where are the orphans' parents? Griffin wondered. Whether they had been killed, sent to debtor's prison, or even sent to live elsewhere, Griffin didn't know. There were too many possibilities.

As he stared at the gray buildings and scared-looking children, Griffin realized that the entire city of London had changed in a mere moment. A web of shadows had descended upon it, and the people were flies, trapped and numbed by poison.

They passed scene after scene of criminal destruction, and

as the train wound near Christ Church, Griffin spotted the cemetery. As the rows of tombstones sped by, his gaze frantically sought out the one monument he hoped not to see.

Please, let Mr. Holmes be still alive, he prayed.

A glowing tomb flickered into view. But where it had once held an epitaph for the world's greatest detective, Griffin now saw that it had been defaced. Someone had taken a hammer to it, and most of the words had crumbled away.

The train let out a long whistle as it sped from the city. To Griffin it sounded like a terrified cry. Throughout the rest of the journey to Stonehenge, he continued to beseech the Creator for courage and guidance. And by the time they finally reached their destination, his fingers ached from where he'd been clenching them together in desperate prayer.

He and his uncle hadn't said a word throughout the entire journey, and even though the trip lasted only a couple of hours, it felt like it had taken weeks to get there.

As the train stopped, Griffin and Rupert leapt from their seats. Without a word they grabbed their packs and checked their weapons. Spurred on by a sense of terror and anxiety like never before, they hurried from the train and hailed the first cab they saw, urging the driver to the ancient monument with as much speed as his horses could muster.

As they raced away into the countryside, Griffin could only hope that time would truly be on their side.

STONEHENGE

The ancient stones at twilight were a sight to behold. Rising from the grassy field like gigantic broken teeth, the site held an air of eerie foreboding. It was no wonder, Griffin thought, that Professor Moriarty and Nigel had chosen such a place to hide their new base of operations. There was something definitely unsettling about it, something that Griffin couldn't help but describe as feeling *evil*.

"All right, boy," Snodgrass said. "What now?"

Griffin stared at his uncle blankly. To his surprise, he realized that he hadn't thought that far in advance.

He turned his gaze to the mammoth stones, noting how they cast elongated shadows. The ring of stones definitely resembled a watch face or some kind of ancient sundial. And as he stared at them, watching as the last ray of the sinking sun struck one of the stones, something occurred to him.

"The center stone!" Griffin exclaimed.

"What?" Rupert replied, looking confused.

"Uncle, your lock picks! Quickly!"

Using his walking stick, Griffin hurried forward as fast as he could, watching how the last beam of light traveled along a stone standing directly across from where it set.

To his credit, Rupert had spent enough time with his nephew to know that Griffin was onto something. He quickly took a bunch of lock picks from a secret pocket inside of his jacket and raced after his nephew.

Griffin bent close to the stone, studying its surface as the thin beam of light traveled along its length. He gazed intently at what looked like a row of tiny notches carved into the stone. The minute he'd thought of a sundial, the idea that there would be some kind of measuring system to count down the minutes at the end of the day had struck him.

The tiny grooves were almost imperceptible, but they were there. They occurred at regular intervals up and down the mammoth rock. He watched, holding his breath as the sunlight inched down to the final groove. Seconds later, when the beam of light touched the final mark, he noticed a tiny shadow, almost invisible, cast to the right of the final minute of the day.

"There!" he cried. "Quick, before it vanishes!"

And Rupert, who had been watching as closely as his nephew, knew what he wanted him to do. The depression in the stone was much newer than the minute markings, but so artistically hidden that nobody would have known where to look. It was a tiny keyhole. And Rupert managed to insert his lock pick just before the light disappeared.

After a few deft turns, Griffin's uncle managed to find the right combination. There was a satisfying *click* as the lock turned. But there was no evidence of a hidden door anywhere on the giant rock. Griffin and Rupert stared at each other, their pale faces looking ghostly in the gathering gloom.

"I wonder where—" Griffin began.

But his words were interrupted by a low rumble. Then the ground began to tremble beneath them. Griffin and Rupert stepped back, watching as the mammoth stone, a piece of rock that must have weighed countless tons, slowly turned on its axis and revealed a staircase descending beneath it.

Griffin gave his uncle a triumphant grin, his white teeth flashing in the newly risen moonlight. Rupert smiled back, feeling a surge of pride at his nephew's cleverness.

"Well done, lad!" Rupert whispered. Griffin beamed at the compliment. He'd learned to treasure words of praise from his uncle, for they were few and far between.

Rupert reached into his pack and removed a small metal box. Then he turned a wind-up key, and a faint beam of greenish light issued from it, bathing the steps below in an eerie glow.

"The Snodgrass Candleless Lantern," his uncle said, responding to his nephew's stunned expression. "Works on phosphorus. Follow close and stay on your guard."

Rupert turned and descended the stone steps.

And as Griffin stood at the entrance, his Scorpion drawn and at the ready, his imagination got the better of him. In the shaky green light, the pale steps resembled teeth, and the darkness ahead reminded him of the throat of some terrible, ancient monster. He closed his eyes for a moment, whispered a short prayer, and then followed his uncle down toward the blackness below.

As they went down, down, down the seemingly endless stairs, Griffin tried not to panic. *One . . . two . . . three . . .* , he counted, trying to calm himself down. But for some reason, this time the counting didn't work. Perhaps the weight of Holmes's death was too great or the thought of meeting Nigel Moriarty too frightening, but Griffin Sharpe could find no comfort in the oppressive darkness beneath the ancient stones.

THE TUNNELS BELOW

Griffin had just counted his two hundred and thirty-seventh stair and was beginning to wonder if the winding staircase would ever come to a stop, when he finally set foot on a flat surface. He breathed a huge sigh of relief. With the exception of the pale beam cast by the Snodgrass Candleless Lantern, everything around them was dark. Griffin sniffed, noticing that the air was dank and smelled faintly of mold. He pushed away images of dead things and creepy tombs from his mind, trying desperately to keep himself calm.

"Where do we go next?" Griffin whispered.

"Not sure," Rupert admitted. The lantern beam only illuminated a path about ten feet ahead. Rupert raised the light and shone it upward, and Griffin could just make out the ceiling of the tunnel. Tiny eyes glittered in the darkness. *Bats*, Griffin thought as goose bumps erupted on his arms and neck.

The passageway ahead was very straight, and the paving stones had been very carefully cut, each one measuring twenty by twenty inches across. Griffin anxiously continued his counting, keeping track of each one as they went.

They'd traveled for about five minutes when a noise ahead made them stop. It sounded to Griffin like two pieces of metal banging together.

"What was that?" Griffin whispered, his voice sounding overly loud in the still air.

"Against the wall!" Rupert hissed. Griffin scrambled to the side of the tunnel and, following his uncle's example, pressed himself against it.

With a click, Rupert doused his lantern. The entire tunnel was plunged into pitch darkness. The sound they'd heard before split the air again, this time much closer. Griffin's heart thudded in his chest, wondering what in the world could have made such a sound. He suddenly wished he could be anywhere else.

There was a rustle next to him as Rupert felt around in his pack. Then Griffin's uncle pushed something down over his eyes. To his amazement, he found that he could see in the dark.

"Snodgrass All-Seeing Spectacles," Rupert hissed in his ear. "The charge only lasts about thirty seconds. Get your Scorpion ready, boy. When it comes near, fire!"

"B-but what am I firing at?" Griffin stammered.

"A deadly machine," Rupert said. "I caught a glimpse of it at the end of the tunnel."

"How did you—?" Griffin began. But then he saw his uncle indicate a strange-looking telescope that was mounted on his rifle.

"No time to explain. Here it comes!"

Griffin looked up, and through the remarkable lenses of the All-Seeing Spectacles, he spotted the machine his uncle had mentioned.

It was black and reminded him of a giant crab or, worse

still, an immense spider. Big, deadly-looking pincers snapped together, making the metal clanking sound that Griffin had heard earlier. Like a crab, the machine moved on multiple legs, but whether it had a pilot concealed beneath the tinted dome on top of it, Griffin couldn't tell.

It moved down the tunnel toward them. Griffin didn't know whether it could see them or not, but it marched steadily forward, directly to the spot where they were trying to hide, with its dangerous-looking claws extended as if with deadly purpose.

Griffin reached for his pistol, his hands nervously fumbling with the holster snap. *Stay calm*, he warned himself. But it was hard to keep his hands from shaking with the *thing* approaching.

The machine was just thirty feet away when Griffin raised his weapon and pointed directly at it.

"Now, boy! Now!" Rupert shouted.

Griffin aimed, steadying his hands as best as he could, and squeezed the trigger.

FLASH! The same blinding light as before exploded in his vision. Even with his eyes squeezed shut, the dancing orbs were imprinted on his retinas. When he opened them again, he saw, with the aid of the spectacles, that the place where the machine had been just moments before was empty. Even with the spots still dancing in his vision, he could clearly see that all that remained was a slightly smoking patch of paving stones.

The thirty-second charge on his spectacles expired, and everything went dark again. As his uncle reignited his lantern, Griffin couldn't help glancing skyward, hoping that the gigantic machine had been transported to somewhere other than above them, unlike his uncle's oilcan.

In the eerie glow Griffin saw the satisfied expression on his uncle's face. He was evidently happy with the way his invention had performed.

"W-where did it go?" Griffin asked.

"Don't know," came his uncle's reply. "But it's no longer our problem. Come on," he said as he moved forward down the tunnel.

Griffin, his heart still racing, followed once more. He didn't particularly like his new weapon and missed his old Stinger. To have been saved from immediate danger was a relief, but Griffin couldn't shake his guilt. He wondered where the terrible machine had gone, and what unsuspecting victim it might prey upon next!

He told himself that he wouldn't use the gun again unless he absolutely had to, and maybe not even then.

Thankfully, they didn't run into any more of the deadly mechanical monsters. The tunnel twisted and turned for many hundreds of paces, but Griffin couldn't see any sign of habitation. If it wasn't for the fact that the spider-like machine had borne the unmistakable design and craftsmanship of Nigel Moriarty, Griffin would have wondered if they had perhaps stumbled upon the wrong place.

"Where is everybody?" Griffin asked.

"Hmm?" replied Snodgrass.

"Isn't it strange that we haven't run into more machines or any guards?" Griffin remarked. "It seems too easy."

"Well, I wouldn't call that thing we just defeated 'easy,'" Snodgrass said with a sniff. "Besides, from the look of things, they weren't expecting visitors. In my opinion, the mechanical device we just ran into was probably instructed to patrol the area as a precaution. I believe we have the entire place to ourselves."

But in spite of his uncle's confidence, Griffin wasn't sure. It just didn't make sense to him that any hideout of the Moriartys' would be so empty. Back in the tunnels beneath the Thames River, the last place that the Moriartys had been hiding out, the place had been swarming with guards.

A thought suddenly occurred to Griffin. Turning to his uncle, he said, "Did you happen to keep the paper we looked at on the train?"

"As a matter of fact, I did," Rupert said, withdrawing the front page from his coat pocket. "I hoped to peruse it later for any additional clues."

Griffin took the paper from his uncle and studied the headline. His face paled as he read the time and date of the ceremony to make Nigel Moriarty England's new prime minister.

"It's today," he said. "No wonder we haven't run into more guards. Everyone must be in London for the ceremony."

"Hmmm," Snodgrass said. "If that's the case, then we need to keep our guard up. They may have left some other safeguards in place to protect against prying eyes. Vigilance!"

But after about an hour of wandering down the tunnel, even Griffin had to admit that it seemed as if they were in no immediate danger. They didn't run into any guards—mechanical or human—and there weren't any hidden traps.

When the light from his uncle's lantern fell on an elegant wooden door at the end of the long, winding passageway, Griffin had let his guard down so much that he nearly opened the door without thinking.

"Wait!" his uncle warned. Then, after rummaging through his pack, he removed what looked like a doctor's stethoscope. Attached to the bell-shaped part at the bottom was a complicated mass of wires and clockwork gears.

After motioning for silence, Rupert pressed the device to the door and put the listening parts in his ears. After a few moments he nodded, looking satisfied.

"I heard someone breathing," he whispered. "There's definitely someone on the other side of this door."

Griffin's hand went automatically to his Scorpion. It made sense that the Moriartys had left someone behind to guard the premises.

Rupert removed his lock picks and set to work on the door's lock, moving the picks with expertise. Soon after, there was a small but definite *click*.

Griffin tried to keep his breathing calm and steady as his uncle counted down with his fingers from three to one. Then, with a sudden twist of the knob, Rupert threw open the door and the two of them rushed inside.

A DASH OF PEPPER

G riffin didn't blink an eye when they entered the sumptuous quarters behind the door. He knew from being around his enemies before that they were individuals who craved elegance and fine furnishings. And the fact that such a beautiful place existed beneath an ancient British monument was of no surprise to him either. It was in keeping with the modus operandi of the Moriartys and what he would have expected. As he scanned the room, he saw no one. But something that didn't quite fit did catch his attention.

On the cushion of a chair in the corner of the room was a small bag made of a material he'd never seen before. Without a second thought, he limped directly to the chair to inspect it.

He stared at what seemed to be the name of a bookseller, printed in outlandish, gaudy colors. He felt the bag, which was made of some kind of artificial material, and tried to assess what it was. Rubber? No. But it was made from something like it.

He opened it and found inside a small rectangular piece of paper. He deduced that it was some sort of receipt. Printed upon it, along with the name of the bookseller, were numbers and possibly codes, and the price of an unspecified book purchased for . . . *twelve pounds sixpence*! It was a huge amount of money. It must be a very valuable book, indeed.

He folded the bag and placed it and the piece of paper in his pocket. He didn't know exactly what he'd found, but felt certain that it was a clue of some kind.

Then he noticed a door at one end of the room that was slightly ajar. He moved toward it, his cane tapping lightly on the stone floor. Rupert, who had spotted the door and was already moving toward it himself, had his rifle drawn. Griffin took note and paused long enough to draw his Scorpion.

But when they opened the door, neither of them was prepared for the extraordinary sight that met their eyes.

"Miss Pepper!" Griffin said.

He looked around the prison cell in which Charlotte Pepper was being kept, noting the heavy iron bars, the long chains that were on her wrists and legs, and worst of all, the black and blue bruises that covered her hands and cheeks. She was dirty and looked as if she hadn't been eating very much. In spite of his anger at her betrayal, Griffin couldn't help feeling sorry for her.

To their surprise, Miss Pepper looked excited to see them. "You came!" she exclaimed, rushing forward as much as her chains would allow.

"Well, well, a bird in a cage," Rupert quipped through gritted teeth. "A criminal of your caliber, *Miss* Pepper, deserves nothing less. In fact, were it up to me, I think a hanging would be more in order."

Charlotte did not meet Rupert's gaze. She stared down at the stone floor of her cell, looking remorseful. It was then that Griffin noticed the glittering spider ring on the third finger of her left hand, the same exact design as the one they'd found clenched in Sherlock Holmes's hand in Sussex. It also matched the size and shape of the lump he'd noticed underneath her silk gloves when she had been at their apartment earlier.

"She's a thief," Griffin said quietly. "But I doubt that she knew that stealing the time machine would lead to the death of Sherlock Holmes. That wasn't your plan, was it, Miss Pepper?"

"What?" said Snodgrass.

"She is wearing a spider-shaped ring," Griffin explained. "But it's not the same one we found on Sherlock Holmes's body. Do you know who was behind the murder, Miss Pepper?"

Charlotte's head snapped up at the mention of the great detective.

"Sherlock Holmes is dead?" Charlotte asked. Griffin read the expression of surprise and horror on her face, and it only confirmed his suspicion that she was innocent of that particular crime.

"He died yesterday," Griffin explained gently. "He'd been poisoned by a ring that looks very much like the one you're wearing now."

Charlotte gazed down at her own ring and frowned. "My ring contains a hypnotic agent, not poison . . ." Then a look of realization crossed her face.

"Atrax," was all she said.

Griffin wasn't sure, but he assumed that Atrax was probably the name of the ring's owner.

Then Charlotte Pepper looked at Rupert and said urgently, "Nigel Moriarty killed Atrax, one of the most dangerous of the Black Widow assassins. He must have taken her ring and used it to murder Sherlock Holmes." Charlotte groaned. "I know the ring you describe, and it's filled with deadly venom from a particular Australian spider."

She gazed up at them, her face twisted with fear. "You must use the time machine to stop Moriarty. He and the professor have done so much damage already. I know where they keep the machine. He recently returned from a trip to the future. He and the professor are both in London now, but I'm certain that they'll be back soon, after the ceremony to make Nigel—"

"Prime minister," Rupert finished for her. "We know already."

Griffin noticed how terrified Charlotte Pepper looked. It was so different from the calm and self-assured woman they'd met on Baker Street. Something had definitely changed about her since he'd last seen her. And Griffin had a hunch that her motives in stealing his uncle's time machine might have been a little different from what he'd read in the note she'd left behind.

"And why should we trust you?" Rupert said with a sneer. "It seems to me that you've done nothing but lie since the moment we met."

"You're right," she said. "If I were in your shoes, I would probably say the same." She gazed at them intently, as if willing them to believe what she was about to say. "But please believe me now. I never would have stolen your time machine if my sister's life were not at stake."

Griffin was taken aback. "What happened to your sister?" he asked.

"Six months ago my parents inherited a ranch in America—California, to be exact. They left England, and I was to look after Mary and then join them after a few weeks."

Charlotte sighed. "But then we were robbed. Someone

broke into our flat and stole the steamship tickets and all of our money. We've been trying to contact our parents but haven't been able to reach them."

Griffin saw tears spring into Miss Pepper's eyes. "We had to find work. We've been trying to save as much as we could, but it's been slow. I've always been good with numbers and found employment with an accountant. Mary took a job working for Sherlock Holmes. She became one of his 'irregulars,' children in his employ who often acted as his eyes and ears around London. They could often go places where a famous detective couldn't."

She wiped her eyes and composed herself. "Mary was one of his best. She's a tough girl . . . even the boys were afraid to pick a fight with her. She's always been kind of a tomboy, but working the streets made her even tougher. She really misses our parents but she doesn't show it by crying. Ever since they left, her reckless spirit has gotten worse. It's made her take on assignments that were too dangerous for her."

"What happened?" Griffin asked.

Miss Pepper took a deep breath. "She ran afoul of the Black Widows, a deadly society of female assassins that Professor Moriarty sometimes hires to do work for him."

"Ah," said Griffin. "So that's where the spider rings fit into all this."

"Precisely," Charlotte said. "Every member wears the ring on her left hand, like a wedding band." She indicated her finger with the glittering ring. "It's largely symbolic, but all of the women in the group have lost their husbands in strange, unexplained circumstances."

Griffin couldn't help wondering if the husbands had been murdered by their assassin wives. He suppressed a shudder. Was

Charlotte one of them? And if so, had she once been married?

His dark thoughts were interrupted as Charlotte continued. "We had nearly saved enough money for steamship tickets when Mary thought that she'd found the Widows' London hideout. She told me that she was going to go back one more time to confirm it and to draw a map."

Charlotte wrung her hands. "Mary felt that Mr. Holmes would have appreciated, and perhaps paid a little extra, for her diligence. We both hoped that his payment for the information would give us the last bit we needed to get to America. But when she didn't return, I assumed the worst . . . The Black Widows must have captured her."

"But you're obviously one of them!" Snodgrass interrupted. "You've got one of the rings yourself!" He turned to Griffin. The boy saw that his uncle's face was red and blotchy with suppressed anger. "Come along, nephew. This woman cannot be trusted. We can find the machine without her help."

Rupert turned to leave, but Griffin stayed behind. He wanted to hear the rest of her story. He could tell that Charlotte Pepper wasn't lying. He'd studied faces long enough to notice the usual habits that went along with deception and could observe none of them as she told them her story.

"Please, Uncle, could we stay a moment?" he asked.

"Whatever for?" Snodgrass snapped.

"I think we should hear the rest of her story. There might be something in it that could help us."

Taking the resigned expression on his uncle's face as permission to stay, Griffin turned back to Charlotte Pepper. "Please go on," Griffin said softly.

Charlotte took a deep breath and said, "It turned out that

I was right. The Widows had captured her and they wouldn't let Mary go. They wanted to get information about Sherlock Holmes and how much he knew about their operation. I am a great admirer of Mr. Holmes and have read all about his cases in the *Strand*. So when Mary didn't come home, I decided to do a little detective work of my own. I was able to piece together where she'd gone and decided to try to save her."

She paused, and Griffin could tell by her pained expression that the memory wasn't pleasant. After a moment she said, "I . . . did research. By going to the most unsavory parts of London, probing the back alleys and searching through the beggars' dens, I was able to discover, bit by bit, who the Black Widows were and how to join them."

She shuddered. "There certainly has never been a more deadly and terrible gathering of women. Most of the people I approached were too afraid to even mention their name."

Griffin held his breath, riveted by her words. Charlotte continued, her gaze distant with memory. "In a dark, forgotten alley, I finally found the person I was looking for. The old woman looked as if she'd survived a fire of some kind. She was terrible in every respect and, most importantly, she was the Widows' gatekeeper."

Griffin saw Miss Pepper's hands shake a little as she continued her account.

"I would have been too frightened to go any further, but my love for Mary compelled me onward. I told the hag that I wanted to join the Black Widows and made up a story about having murdered my husband. It was the first requirement for admittance into their organization. Only a woman who had murdered her spouse would be considered."

"How did you convince them that you had done it?" Griffin asked. "Didn't they check to see if you were telling the truth?"

Charlotte glanced at him. "I studied the obituaries until I found an unsolved murder, then claimed responsibility for it." She shrugged. "It was enough to get me through the door. But what came next . . ."

She winced at the memory. "Well, I had . . . had no idea what they do to their initiates. If I had, I don't think I would have had the strength to do it in the first place. I was tortured in terrible ways, forced to endure the pain of being bitten by several deadly spiders."

Griffin's eyes widened. Charlotte spoke softly, her voice barely a whisper. "Just before the point of death, an antidote was delivered. I was allowed to recover only enough to be bitten again. It was terrible . . ."

If Rupert Snodgrass was listening to Miss Pepper's account, he was trying very hard to give no outward signs. But Griffin did notice his uncle shift uncomfortably at the mention of the spiders. To endure such treatment must have been torture indeed!

"I finally found out the location of where my sister was being kept. Moriarty has a special prison beneath the Tower of London where he keeps his kidnapping victims. It's an awful place, filled with rats, and worse. The only person who has a key is the professor himself. So when the Widows told me that he'd hired them for a new mission, one that involved close contact with him, I had to take it."

She gave Griffin a sorrowful look. "I should have known better than to try to act the double agent. The professor is as cunning as Sherlock Holmes, but uses his reasoning abilities for dark purposes. He found out that I wasn't really a Black Widow, for I had never been married. He checked the church records."

"Clever," Griffin admitted.

"I knew that after I fulfilled my mission to steal the time machine and deliver it to Stonehenge, he would probably tell the others. The penalty for betraying the Widows is death. So I decided to leave the note in your apartment, one that I filled with subtle clues, hoping that it would lead you here."

She looked up at Griffin and Rupert and offered them a small smile. "And here you are," she finished. "I've been hoping and praying that you would rescue me, but I know I don't deserve it. And you don't have to—just please rescue Mary. I'm truly sorry for stealing your machine. I have to admit, until I saw Nigel use it, I didn't think that it would actually work."

She glanced over at Rupert and gave him a wistful smile. "I'm afraid I underestimated your genius, Mr. Snodgrass. I had no idea that anyone really could have found a way to travel through time. I thought that the professor was chasing a pipe dream, and that once he had the machine, he would discover that it didn't really work. Had I known what terrible uses he and Nigel wanted it for, I would have never, ever delivered it into their hands. May God forgive me for what I've done."

She began to weep quietly. Rupert gazed down at the woman with a slightly less hostile expression. Griffin could tell that her story had impacted him. But he knew his uncle wasn't one to forgive quickly.

Griffin felt a surge of compassion for Miss Pepper and all of the terrible things she'd gone through to rescue her sister. He could imagine how difficult her decision had been, to join forces with an evil organization so that she could save someone she loved. Her solution hadn't been the right way to handle the problem, but she had done it for the right reasons. And he did feel that she was finally being honest with them.

He couldn't undo her actions, but he could offer her forgiveness for the deception and theft of the time machine. He reached his small hand through the bars and gently stroked her bruised fingers.

"All's forgiven, Miss Charlotte," Griffin said. Then, glancing up at Rupert, he added, "Right, Uncle?"

Rupert Snodgrass muttered something unintelligible, but Griffin was pleased to notice that he did remove the lock picks from his pocket. Seeing a chance for freedom, Charlotte's eyes brightened.

"You'll set me free?"

"Yes, but we will need your help. We can still put matters to rights. After we get the machine, then maybe we can find a way to stop whatever Nigel Moriarty has done to affect the present. I assume that he's found some kind of information by traveling through time, something that has helped him and his uncle gain power. Then we can rescue your sister," Griffin said.

But as soon as Rupert placed his lock picks into the lock, his face grew concerned. He twisted, prodded, and poked at the lock, but it wouldn't budge. His arms strained with exertion and tiny beads of sweat appeared on his forehead, but after a considerable effort, he finally stopped, obviously frustrated and at his wits' end.

"Custom lock," Rupert explained. "It can't be picked.".

A sudden booming noise startled them. Griffin jumped. The terrible sound of one of the clanking metal spiders echoing from somewhere outside in the tunnels mingled with the sound of rough voices. Someone was coming!

"Leave me!" Charlotte hissed. "If they find you here, you're done for! Your machine is through that door and in a chamber to the left. GO!"

"But what about you?" Snodgrass said. And Griffin noticed that all traces of bitterness were gone. He gazed at Miss Pepper with a look of deep concern, and the woman was obviously touched by his attention.

She reached through the bars as best as she could with her chained hands. Rupert moved his to hers, and the two of them gazed into each other's eyes.

"Not everything I said was a lie, you know," Charlotte said. She smiled gently. "You truly are the most gifted inventor I've ever met and a wonderful man too. I . . . I wish circumstances had been different. I would have liked very much to know you better."

Rupert melted. He brushed Miss Pepper's bruised fingers with his lips, a gallant gesture Griffin had never seen his uncle make before—had never dreamed his uncle *could* make before. And then, with tears in his eyes, Griffin's uncle said, "I will see to it that we have that opportunity, dear lady. We will use the time machine to return and set you free."

Charlotte blushed. "If anyone can do it, I'm certain that you can. But for now, I'm afraid it's off to the Tower of London for me. Good luck, Mr. Snodgrass—"

"Rupert, please," Griffin's uncle said.

And then, hearing footsteps outside the door, Griffin pulled at his uncle's sleeve, urging him to depart.

Griffin's cane tapped in quick clicks as he moved across the stone floor with his uncle close behind. As they dashed through the walnut door at the end of the room, Griffin heard a rough voice behind him call out, "Stop or we'll shoot!"

Griffin's breath caught in his throat and he almost turned around, but he knew they had to keep going. Even as bullets ricocheted behind them, Griffin and Rupert dashed for the thing for which they'd come.

If we can just get to the time machine and stop Moriarty from doing whatever he did, all of this will go away, Griffin thought.

And everyone, including Sherlock Holmes and Miss Pepper, will be saved!

TIME-TRAVELING TEAPOT

Griffin plunged through the second door, narrowly avoiding a hail of gunfire. He froze when he saw his uncle bending over an elegant pedestal. Nigel Moriarty was not only a criminal genius but also an incredible artist and engineer. The pedestal on which the time machine teapot was displayed was remarkably beautiful, with a custom-fitted silken pillow on top of it to house Rupert's invention.

"I can't tell which way he went," Rupert said anxiously. "The machine has three settings: past, present, and future. There's no way to tell how far into either direction he traveled."

"Uncle, I think you should just choose one!" Griffin shouted. He could hear the approaching footsteps of their enemies pounding down the corridor behind them. "We haven't any time!"

"Oh, I disagree. We have all the *time* in the world!" Rupert muttered. He threw a switch on the side of the teapot and extended his hand to Griffin. "Take my hand!" he said.

And as Griffin felt the firm grip of his uncle's hand, a blaze of swirling light erupted from the top of the teapot and exploded around him. He could hear the door behind him swing open and the angry shouts of Moriarty's henchmen.

Then the world around him completely changed, and he found himself pulled out of his very existence. The sensation felt almost like someone had reached down and pulled him up by the roots of his hair, only there was no pain at all. And the next thing he knew, he found himself flying through a long tunnel of light and sound.

Prior to its happening, Griffin hadn't thought much about what time traveling would look or feel like, but even in his wildest imaginations, he never would have expected the experience to create music.

A melodic warbling, almost like the sound of a pipe organ or calliope, seemed to be all around him. It was a beautiful melody, impossible to describe, but one that brought to mind swirling space and gently turning planets.

He felt a sense of tremendous peace.

Then, almost as suddenly as it had begun, he felt the lights around him begin to change. The feeling of being pulled grew weaker, and gradually a brand-new environment spread out in front of him.

Moriarty's underground lair had changed.

Instead of an elegant parlor, Griffin found himself in an empty underground chamber. There was a tiny bit of light, made from flickering torches set at regular intervals down a long corridor of dirt and rock.

"Where are we?" Griffin asked.

Rupert stood beside him, looking pale and uncertain in the flickering torchlight. "What you mean is, *when* are we?" Rupert replied.

Griffin noticed that his uncle's knuckles were white as they gripped the teapot's handle. But then Rupert's anxious expression suddenly changed from concern to excitement. He grinned, gazing around at the dirt and rock.

"Do you realize what this means?" he exclaimed, staring down the passageway that led from the empty room. "I've done it. I've really done it." He looked down at his nephew with a triumphant smile on his lips. "Welcome to the future, my boy!"

Griffin smiled back. It was great to see his uncle so happy. And it really was awe inspiring to think about. To actually have traveled through time! Griffin shook his head in disbelief. It was completely surreal, and there was no doubt about it—his uncle truly was a genius!

"What year do you think we've arrived in?" Griffin asked.

"No way to be certain," Rupert replied. "As I said before, the device doesn't have the ability to navigate to a particular point in time."

"But if that's the case, how can we possibly hope to arrive at the same time and place as Nigel Moriarty? We could be hundreds of years off!"

"True," Rupert admitted. "But since time is irrelevant when using this device, we can always go back into the past and keep trying until we get there."

Griffin groaned inwardly. Jumping back and forth through time and hoping to get lucky enough to arrive at the same time and date as Nigel Moriarty seemed almost impossible. Griffin assumed that Moriarty had traveled to the future, because he had used whatever information he'd gathered there to affect the present. But then again, what if he had traveled to the past and used his present knowledge to affect the time that they were currently in?

The prospect of trying to figure it all out gave Griffin a headache. But at least they had managed to escape Moriarty's henchmen and were currently in possession of the time machine. It gave them the upper hand, and he hoped they would discover a way to use their advantage wisely.

As they walked down the tunnel that led out of the chamber, Griffin noticed that the pathway was laid out differently from the way it had been when they had first entered.

Rupert didn't seem to notice. He was excitedly rambling about how his time machine would change the world and how everyone would finally give him the recognition he so richly deserved.

Griffin didn't have the heart to mention that Rupert's machine already had changed the world, and not in a good way. So he kept silent, letting his uncle savor his triumph.

After following the torch-lit passage for several hundred yards, Rupert and Griffin came to an ancient-looking staircase. Unlike the one that had led downward from underneath the monolithic stone, this one twisted upward to a clear opening in the earth.

"Hmm, future generations must have found this place," Rupert muttered as they climbed upward. "But I wonder why they didn't install handrails."

Griffin had been wondering something along the same lines. If this was indeed the future, why did everything look so primitive? He wouldn't have expected future generations to still be using torches to light passageways.

This thought had just occurred to him when they exited the tunnel and found themselves standing in a cave opening surrounded by tall pine trees. A cool evening breeze rustled the branches and brought with it a fresh-smelling fragrance. The stars blazed overhead, and in the distance Griffin could make out what looked like a campfire somewhere in the vicinity of the huge Stonehenge monoliths.

Rupert saw it too and said, "Perhaps they have turned Stonehenge into a campsite for tourists. Let's go see if whoever's there can help us discover precisely what year this is and what kind of transportation we can get to London."

As they made their way through the woods, a task made a bit more difficult for Griffin because his walking stick kept sinking into the damp earth, the fire from the campsite grew larger. In fact, as they got closer to it, they realized it wasn't a small campfire at all. It was a huge, roaring bonfire.

Griffin could make out silhouettes moving in front of the flames. They seemed to be wearing long robes and dancing.

And that was when it suddenly hit him. Those figures were definitely not campers, and this was not the future.

"Uncle?"

"Hmm?" Snodgrass replied, still walking toward the big bonfire. He seemed unconcerned about the strange figures, probably assuming that in the future anything could be possible.

"Uncle, I think we'd better not get any closer," Griffin whispered.

"Why?"

"I don't think those are campers," Griffin explained.

"Nonsense!" Rupert boomed. Griffin winced at how loud his uncle's voice sounded.

The figures, who were now fewer than twenty yards away, suddenly stopped their dance. As they turned and stared at the spot where Griffin and his uncle were standing, Griffin could clearly see their dark cloaks and long hoods and knew them now for precisely what they were.

Griffin grabbed his uncle's arm. "We're not in the future; we're in the Iron Age! Those people are druids, and they are not going to want us here!"

"What?" Rupert replied, appearing confused. "You're wrong. This is the future! I set the switch on the machine myself!" He glanced back down at the teapot, inspecting the switch.

The tallest of the dark-robed figures let out a cry in a language Griffin couldn't understand. Suddenly, all the rest withdrew long daggers from beneath their cloaks.

"Well, whatever you did, it didn't work!" Griffin said. "Let's get out of here!"

Snodgrass fiddled with the knob on the side of the time machine, oblivious to the danger they were in. Griffin watched as the cloaked figures marched toward them, knives extended. If they didn't do something quick, they were literally history!

Griffin, seeing no other way, reached over and grabbed the switch on the teapot. He toggled it back and forth for a moment, hoping that it would jar the machine into moving in the proper direction. Then he threw the switch forward to the spot marked "Future," and the world around them began to spin with flashing lights once more.

He saw the cloaked figures hesitate. But then, at a command from their leader, they leapt forward, shouting and brandishing their weapons. Perhaps it was because what they were seeing looked like magic to them, or for some other reason; Griffin couldn't tell. But rather than being frightened, they seemed intent upon attack.

Hurry! Griffin thought as the lights swirled faster. They still hadn't disappeared, and the druids were just a few feet away. He saw a glittering blade rise, and the cloak of one of the nearest attackers fell back, revealing a pale face twisted in rage.

The knife swung down just as Griffin felt the familiar pulling sensation jerk him off his feet. There was the sound of cloth tearing in the vicinity of his trouser leg, and then everything turned back into the chorus of unearthly music and brilliant light.

MISS FITCH

When the lights cleared for the second time, the first thing Griffin noticed was that it was no longer night. Warm sunshine was all around him, and the gigantic stones were devoid of any angry tribesmen.

Griffin breathed a sigh of relief and gazed down at his trouser leg, which was, as he suspected, torn at the bottom. The knife had just missed his good leg by a few inches. If it had struck, it would have been the second time he had been wounded in such a way.

After breathing a quick prayer of thanks, he leaned on his stick and gazed around at the grassy plain surrounding Stonehenge. It appeared to be deserted.

Glancing over at his uncle, he saw that he was muttering angrily as he examined his machine, checking it for damage. He turned to Griffin and growled, "What do you think you were doing back there? You could have broken the knob off twisting it back and forth like that!"

"I'm sorry, Uncle. We were out of time—they were going to attack us. I thought that maybe some part of it had failed to engage the last time we used it and maybe jiggling it a little would put it right," Griffin said.

Rupert gave an irritated snort. "That is not the proper way to handle delicate equipment, nor is it very scientific! The next time you get an idea like that into that oversized brain of yours, ask me first!"

"All right, I will," Griffin said contritely. He realized that his uncle had a point. What if he had broken the machine? They could have been stuck anywhere in time without a way back!

They walked across the grass toward a strangely paved road. Everything was even and flat—no cobblestones or dirt. Griffin could tell, even at a distance, that whatever had been used to make the road hinted at future technology. Rupert concluded that it had been made of some kind of hardened tar, an ingenious way to produce a smooth and traversable surface.

Suddenly, a roaring sound caused both of them to look up. Hurtling toward them at an incredible speed was something that looked to them like a silver carriage. It squealed to a stop just inches from where both of them stood, staring dumbfounded at the futuristic-looking machine.

A door slid open on hidden hinges, and a woman stepped out from inside the machine. "Whateryoudoin,tryintocausean accident?"

Griffin couldn't make out the woman's rapid speech at first. It sounded like English, but it was spoken so quickly he couldn't figure out what she'd said.

"Excuse me?" he replied with a blush.

Griffin noticed that the woman was dressed in a most scandalous fashion. All that she wore was a loose-fitting blouse with the words "Abercrombie & Fitch" written upon it and tight-fitting trousers of some kind of stretchy, blue material. Griffin decided that the words, perhaps, were the woman's name.

Griffin tried to look away, feeling embarrassed. He'd never imagined that people in the future would dress like that! Griffin noticed that his uncle was staring at the woman, his mouth gaping.

"I'm sorry . . . Miss . . . ah . . . Fitch," Griffin said. "We're not from around here and were hoping that you might help us."

"Miss Fitch? I'm not . . ." Then she glanced down at her shirt and nodded, noting the name written there.

"Oh, I see. Good one." She said this drily without the least bit of amusement in her voice. Griffin noticed that the woman was chewing something with apparent relish, her jaws moving up and down in a nonstop, rhythmic fashion. A second later she removed a small gray lump of what looked to Griffin like rubber and then, holding it between her scarlet-painted nails, said, "Are you blokes on your way to a Steampunk convention or something? Those are great costumes!"

She glanced amusedly at Griffin's and his uncle's clothing, noting Griffin's tweed cap and walking stick and his uncle's tattered bowler, jacket, and vest.

"Er, no, madam, nothing of the sort," Rupert replied carefully. "We are travelers and new to the area."

"Tourists. I get it. So, what, they don't have roads where you're from? I could have run you over!"

"Yes, well, we're sorry about that," Griffin said awkwardly. "As my uncle said, we are unfamiliar with the area and—"

"Excuse me, but what precisely is the date, may I ask? We're in a bit of a hurry," Rupert said, interrupting his nephew.

The woman plunged the gray, rubbery wad back into her mouth and began chewing loudly. "What?"

"The date, my good woman, the date. What year is this?" Rupert smiled, showing all of his teeth. He spoke slowly and carefully, as if he were addressing a child. Griffin knew that he was trying to be as polite as possible, but had also noticed that in the past his uncle's attempts at good manners didn't often work.

They didn't seem to work in the future either.

"Oh, I get it. You're LARPers," the young woman said with a smile.

Griffin and his uncle exchanged puzzled looks.

"I assure you, madam, we are not on a lark at all," Rupert replied.

"My brother is one too, you know. A 'live action role player'?" She winked. "Always getting together with his little geeky friends and acting out those crazy games." She smiled and rolled her eyes. "Well, you're both very convincing. I would say that your accent is a bit forced, but otherwise not too bad."

She slouched against the door of her silver vehicle. "So, what is this one about, some kind of H. P. Lovecraft or Sherlock Holmes thingy?"

Rupert and Griffin stared at her blankly. They hardly knew what to say. The woman seemed to have drawn her own conclusions about who they were, and she knew something of Holmes. But since doing so, she didn't seem nearly as suspicious as before and had relaxed considerably.

"All right, I'll play along. Got nothin' better to do today anyway. So, where're the others in your group? Are you doing some kind of treasure hunt?"

Griffin saw this statement as an opportunity to finally help them get to where they were going. Smiling back at the woman, and trying not to blush at her scandalous attire, he said, "In a sense, yes, we are on a sort of treasure hunt. Actually, we need to get to London as soon as possible."

"All the way to London? That's over an hour away! Whoever your Game Master is really went to town on this one. Well, hop in, then," she said.

Feeling bewildered but grateful for the assistance, Griffin and his uncle entered the woman's vehicle. As Griffin slid into the backseat of the carriage, he realized that he was sitting in some kind of advanced motorcar.

"Amazing!" he murmured as the woman turned a key and the engine flared to life. Within seconds they were flying back down the interestingly paved road toward London, as fast as the fastest train, with some kind of noise that he assumed was music thumping so loudly in his ears Griffin couldn't even hear himself think!

NEW LONDON

As they rode, Griffin discovered many more incredible things about the future. One thing he observed was that people in the future tried to do way too many things all at once. The woman who drove the car was trying to hold a conversation, steer the motorcar, and type messages into a small rectangular device, all at the same time. And Griffin could tell by the swerving of the car, and the frightened honks of other drivers, that she wasn't doing it very well.

Rupert noted the device and asked the woman about it, and the woman laughed, complimenting him again on his "ability to stay in character."

"It's only a 4G phone," she explained. "I'll be upgrading as soon as I can afford it."

Rupert didn't know what she meant by "4G," but he did brighten considerably when he found out that the tiny device was a telephone that operated without the use of wires. The woman allowed him to look at it, and when he passed it over to Griffin for examination, Griffin was able to get a look at a date that was displayed on its tiny, glowing screen.

5 August 2012.

His mind boggled. They'd traveled over one hundred years into the future! Suddenly, another thought struck him. He reached into his coat pocket and withdrew the slip of paper he'd found in Moriarty's hideout.

He couldn't believe he hadn't noticed it before, but there, printed at the top of the receipt, was a date. A thrill shot through him as he saw what it was!

5 August 2012.

Rupert and the woman were deep in conversation, or about as deep as the woman could manage while doing so many different tasks at once. Her end of the conversation consisted of a lot of grunts, eye rolls, and absentminded comments.

Griffin interrupted. "Excuse me, Uncle," he said.

"Fascinating . . . and what exactly do you mean by this term 'Why Fie'?" Rupert asked, then turning to his nephew before she could answer, said, "What?"

"We've done it!" Griffin said, his eyes shining with excitement. "Look here." He showed his uncle the date on the receipt. "We've arrived on exactly the same date Moriarty was here. I found this at the hideout."

Rupert examined the receipt closely. "By Jove, this is a good turn!" he exclaimed. Then he paused, looking thoughtful. He examined the teapot, taking careful note of the switch that was marked "Past," "Present," and "Future."

"Griffin, when you rattled the switch back and forth, how many times did you do it?" Rupert asked.

Griffin thought back to the woods by Stonehenge, at the moment just before they were attacked.

"Twice," he said.

Rupert nodded excitedly. "I think I know what happened. You completed a circuit. By switching back and forth like that, the interdimensional chrono-apparatus was able to retrieve one of the locations it went to before we used it."

"We've gone to the exact time of Nigel Moriarty's last journey!" Griffin said happily. He pointed at the receipt. "And now that we have the name of the bookstore that he went to, all we have to do is hope that we get there before he shows up."

"Precisely," Snodgrass replied.

"And then you'll win the game, right?" the woman said, smacking the wad in her mouth loudly.

"Er, yes. Sort of," Griffin replied. "By the way, Miss Fitch. May I ask what it is that you are chewing?"

The girl grinned and grabbed a slim cardboard package. Handing it to Griffin, she said, "If you wanted a piece of gum, all you had to do was ask."

Griffin examined the container. Inside were little white rectangles. Feeling very curious, he popped one into his mouth. A delicious taste of mint immediately washed over his tongue and teeth. Griffin chewed, appreciating the consistency.

"This candy is quite good," he said, trying not to smack too loudly. Then, without thinking, he did the thing that seemed to him most natural.

He swallowed.

It was like trying to eat a piece of rubber. After the wad of gum traveled uncomfortably down his throat, Griffin wrinkled his nose and held a hand to his stomach, not enjoying the sensation at all. What kind of terrible candy was this?

"You didn't swallow it, did you?" the girl asked.

Griffin nodded, looking miserable. Miss Fitch chuckled and

shook her head in disbelief. "I don't know where you blokes are from, but you sure are weird."

She eased the car over to a faster lane of traffic.

"Well, we're almost to the city. What was the name of the place you were going to?"

Rupert showed her the receipt, and the young woman used her telephone to punch in the name. Soon afterward, something she called a GPS showed them exact instructions on how to get to the bookstore.

This particular bit of technology was truly amazing to both Griffin and his uncle. It was a wonderful scientific achievement. A person would never feel lost again!

As London grew closer, Griffin stared in awe at the incredible skyline that was and wasn't the London he knew. The tall buildings that nearly touched the clouds, the abundance of motorcars, and the incredible array of shops filled with everything imaginable—and unimaginable—made him feel that this London was hardly the same place in which he'd spent the past summer—and it wasn't, he supposed. Between the changes Moriarty had made and all of the technology like the woman had, it was bound to be quite different indeed.

He saw signs indicating strange and exotic foods . . . whatever, for instance, was a "veggie burger" or a "protein smoothie"? Contemplating this, he realized that he hadn't eaten anything for many hours—or, now that he thought about it, all century!

His stomach growled, loudly enough for the woman to notice. She reached into a box in the car's instrument panel and withdrew a small, brightly wrapped bar.

"Hungry?" she asked.

"Famished, thank you," Griffin replied. The unpleasant effect of the gum in his stomach had worn off, and Griffin found himself eager for a meal. The woman paused while doing the thing she called "texting" long enough to hand him the packet. Griffin read the shiny words printed on the wrapper.

Lo Carb Tofu Energy Bar.

He unwrapped it and gazed down at the lumpy brown thing inside. He wasn't quite sure whether it was food or not, and sniffed it experimentally. It smelled slightly sweet, so he took a small bite.

Griffin had been raised with excellent manners and knew that it was very rude to spit something out once it had been placed inside one's mouth. But it was very hard to resist the temptation to do so. The thing tasted so unlike anything he'd ever eaten that it was all he could do to swallow and then politely hide the rest of the bar in his coat pocket. Even his uncle's favorite dried cod was better than this!

He arrived at a very important conclusion. The food he'd tasted in the future certainly wasn't anywhere as good as Mrs. Tottingham's lemon scones. And Griffin made a mental note to himself not to eat anything else in this strange time and place.

The car pulled to a stop alongside a busy street, and the woman dropped them off outside of the largest bookstore Griffin had ever seen.

"Thank you, Miss Fitch, for your generosity," Griffin said and doffed his cap. The woman laughed and, to his surprise, grabbed him in a quick hug.

"Oh, you're too much," she said, still laughing. And then, after wishing them good luck in finding their treasure, she jumped back into her motorcar and sped off down the street.

Rupert grinned down at his nephew. "Well, this looks like the place!"

Griffin could tell that his uncle seemed delighted by everything he saw. He wished he could feel the same. There was something about the future London he didn't quite like. Perhaps it was the way the people passing by seemed so rushed and unhappy. As he studied the faces of the busy Londoners, not one of them looked as if he or she was friendly. They looked worried and filled with stress.

On the other hand, he noticed that the city's air was cleaner and didn't smell of factory smoke. There weren't any beggars on the street that he could see, and everywhere people held the same small telephones that Miss Fitch had carried and were constantly talking, typing, or caressing them. He sighed. Perhaps it was just too much for him to understand.

Griffin followed his uncle into the incredible bookstore, which had moving stairs that could take a person up four floors! Griffin was overwhelmed by the endless variety of books, and was particularly attracted to a section filled with Bibles and other religious texts.

He paused to look at one of the leather-bound volumes and was surprised to find that the inside contained not a book at all but a small oblong screen. When he pushed a button on the bottom of the screen, the word *eTestament* appeared, and shortly after, a list of all the books of the Bible with their chapters.

Griffin lightly tapped the screen and found the book, chapter, and verse he most loved: Hebrews 13:8.

"Jesus Christ is the same yesterday, today, and forever."

The passage told of constancy, truth, and the persistence of God's love. That it could cross any boundary, including time and space. For Griffin, a boy who loved truth and loved things that made sense, it was a constant reminder that he could trust in one thing that would never fail: Jesus, God's eternal gift of love and salvation. Plus, it was a nice reminder that God was here in the future too.

So it was with a profound sense of relief that he read the familiar and comforting passage. Perhaps he'd been a bit too hasty in assuming that this new and future world was all bad. Whether on a written page or on an illuminated screen, the words were still here. And they were timeless truths that mankind had trusted for generations.

"Over here, boy," he heard his uncle call. Griffin replaced the amazing Bible back on the shelf and hurried over to his uncle. Rupert was standing in line, waiting for a clerk to finish helping other customers. Griffin watched people hand the clerk small, lightweight cards that he slid through a machine. This apparently paid for the item they wished to purchase, for they were given a small, white receipt afterward. Griffin noted that it was exactly the same as the one he'd taken from the Moriartys' lair.

"Excuse me, my good fellow," Rupert said when it was his turn to move ahead in line.

The busy man barely glanced up, but said, "How may I help you?"

"Perhaps you could text this into your adding machine and tell me what was purchased from your shop?" Rupert said, smiling.

Griffin could tell that he was trying his best to sound like the woman in the motorcar, speaking quickly and trying to use the local language. The man raised an eyebrow at the strange request but didn't reply. Instead, he lifted a small device that had a red light within it and brushed it across a series of bars printed on the bottom of the receipt.

"*The Complete Adventures of Sherlock Holmes,*" he said. "I have a copy right here, but you can't buy it. It's been reserved for a book club. Would you like to look at it? We may have another copy upstairs."

"Thank you," Griffin replied, taking the book. He and his uncle stepped aside to leaf through the large hardback book. As he and Rupert scanned the pages, Griffin's mind flashed into overdrive. What could Nigel Moriarty possibly have wanted with such a book? He already knew what had happened in all of the cases—why not just go back and change them? Why did he need the book?

But then, as he came across the cases after 1903, both Griffin and his uncle realized what the evil man had done. It was so subtle and clever only a criminal artist like Nigel would have ever thought of such a thing! Sherlock Holmes had had more adventures, and by stealing the book, Moriarty knew in advance exactly where he'd be and how to ambush him.

It was how he'd found a way to murder the great detective. And Griffin knew that once Holmes was gone, London had opened up for the Moriartys to take over and establish their terrible empire.

"Ah, too bad it's spoken for," Rupert said. "Do you happen to know, my good man, where we could GPS such a book?"

The man stared at him for a moment with a puzzled expression. Then, as if figuring out what he was trying to say, he replied, "GPS? You mean where to find it? Aisle thirty-four, second floor. You'll find it in the bargain bin."

"Thank you!" Rupert enthused. And then, after beaming a

triumphant smile at his nephew, the two set off to navigate the maze of bookshelves and find this "bargain bin" the man had mentioned. Griffin wanted to read up on Sherlock Holmes's future cases as much as his uncle did. It could give them valuable information as to the future (or the present or the past, depending on how you looked at it, Griffin thought) plots and schemes of the Moriartys.

They had just emerged from the moving stairway to the second floor when they spotted a man dressed in the same style of clothing they wore, reaching into a large basket of specially marked books.

At first, Griffin wasn't sure it was him, but when he saw the man's angular features and curled, gray mustache, his blood froze. There was a sharp pain in his leg, a cruel reminder of the terrible wound inflicted upon him by the one person he feared more than any other. It was the first time he'd seen him up close since the fateful day he'd almost been killed by the man's sword. And as he stood there, staring at him not forty feet away, Griffin's heart was filled with dread at the sight of his terrible adversary.

It was, indeed, Nigel Moriarty!

SO CLOSE

Y OU!" Snodgrass yelled.

Nigel Moriarty glanced up, searching for the source of the shout. His eyes narrowed when he saw Rupert and Griffin, then widened perceptibly at the sight of his old walking stick. His eyes flicked to the teapot that Rupert carried and, with a malicious grin, raised its twin in his other hand.

It was a paradox. The fact that the same object from different times could exist simultaneously in the same world seemed impossible. And yet, here they were, a past version of Moriarty and a slightly more recent version of Rupert and Griffin, both in the future, both carrying time machines.

It was too much for Griffin to comprehend, and there was no time for him to think about it. Pushing away the part of his mind that wanted to wrestle with the scientific challenge it proposed, Griffin instead moved to action, drawing his Scorpion and pointing it at his adversary.

"Put the book down, Mr. Moriarty," Griffin called.

Nigel sneered in response. "Or what, boy? You'll shoot me with one of your uncle's silly, 'nonlethal' inventions? Hardly!"

Rupert, who still had his rifle slung on his back, whipped it over his shoulder in one smooth movement. "'Nonlethal' doesn't mean it won't hurt!" he shouted, then pulled the trigger.

What emerged from the tip of the gun looked to Griffin like a swarm of silver bees. In fact, they were something else, something of so cunning and ingenious a design that even Nigel Moriarty would have had to appreciate the artistry that had gone into creating them.

Tiny flying robots, each equipped with a needle-like stinger, flew toward Moriarty with deadly intent. Later, his uncle informed him that, once released, the missile-like drones would follow their target indefinitely, chasing them to whatever destination they ran to, never giving up until they had delivered their poisonous payload . . . a concoction brewed from poison ivy, stinging nettles, and fire ants! Nasty stuff, indeed!

But one thing that the drones couldn't do was follow their prey beyond the present time, and Moriarty was nothing if not quick-minded.

Griffin watched at first with exultation at his uncle's shot but then in horrified despair as Nigel threw the switch on his time machine and the lights around him began to swirl.

Perhaps a few of the drones got there in time, because as Moriarty vanished, Griffin fancied that he could hear cries of pain. But in seconds the man had disappeared and the silver drones, now robbed of their target, fell harmlessly to the ground.

The entire floor of the bookstore had gone from a hive of activity to utter silence. Stunned faces stared at Griffin and Rupert, unable to believe what they'd witnessed. Then suddenly, someone in the crowded store came to his senses and pointed a shaking finger at Rupert, shouting, "He's got a gun!"

"Run, boy!" Rupert exclaimed.

Moving as fast as they could, the two of them shot through the screaming crowd and made their way out the door. Griffin could hear the chaos behind them and soon after heard a terrible wailing alarm. It was a noise that in any time meant the same thing.

The police were coming!

Much about London had changed since 1903. But, thankfully, many of the streets were exactly the same. Griffin and his uncle charged down an alley they recognized, twisted and turned through two others, and emerged on a very familiar street.

As they ran, Griffin's leg felt like it was on fire. He tried to use the cane as much as he could for support and knew that he couldn't keep up the frantic pace his uncle set. But as they turned the corner, he counted down the addresses until he found the one they'd been looking for.

The apartments at 221 Baker Street looked very similar except for two very important details. The first was that 221B, Sherlock Holmes's apartment, now had a sign outside of it that read Sherlock Holmes Museum.

But the second was far worse. Through the years, someone had changed the architecture of Griffin's uncle's residence. For now, right where 221A used to be, was a restaurant.

"What the deuce?" cried Snodgrass. He stared back and forth between the entrance to his apartment and the Sherlock Holmes museum. Griffin could tell right away that the years of hoping that he, Rupert Snodgrass, would someday be famous like Sherlock Holmes had suddenly disappeared in a disappointed *POOF!* Without a doubt, the legacy of Sherlock Holmes would live on throughout history, and the names Rupert Snodgrass and Griffin Sharpe definitely would not.

And knowing that fact made Griffin breathe a sigh of relief. For him, it meant that his plan for remaining the World's Most Secret Detective was working. There would never be a sign, a museum, a monument, or a statue commemorating the place where he'd lived with his uncle. His detective work would forever be a secret.

And that thought gave him a thrill equal to his uncle's disappointment. For if the criminals didn't know who he was or what he looked like, they would never see him coming. Not only that, but he never wanted to be tempted by fame or glory. The work he did, he did simply because it was a gift that the Lord had given him. Nothing more, nothing less. If there was any glory to be had, he wished it to go to God.

"Come along, Uncle," Griffin said sympathetically. "We need to hide, and I can think of no better place than in here. Somewhere where nobody knows who we are."

Rupert's face clouded, and then, quite unexpectedly, he chuckled.

"Quite so." He laughed. Then, placing his arm around his nephew's shoulder, he said, "Oh, dash it all, I'm starving anyway! Who cares about a moldy old museum."

Griffin stared at him for a moment, amazed that he'd gotten over what had to be a great disappointment so quickly. Then, as they walked inside the merry restaurant, Griffin smiled.

Sometimes his uncle Rupert could still surprise him.

A NEW PLAN

After sitting down in the restaurant, they'd been about to order—Griffin's hunger getting the better of his resolution to never eat food from the future again—when Rupert took one look at the prices listed on the menu and let out a gasp.

"Fourteen pounds for fish and chips!" he exclaimed.

Griffin was astonished too. After doing a quick conversion of British pounds to American dollars in his head, he realized that the price of the meal was close to twenty dollars! It was a small fortune in 1903.

He whistled softly. Of course, neither he nor his uncle had brought such an extravagant amount with them.

Rupert proposed that they order and then just use the time machine to go back to their present, but Griffin reminded him that that was stealing and forced his grumbling uncle to reconsider.

They decided they needed a new plan of attack. They'd tried to stop Moriarty from stealing the book in the future and failed. "The only thing to try now is to journey to the past. If we could arrive right here at our apartment on the night that Miss Pepper stole the time machine, maybe we could stop her!" Griffin said.

Rupert looked doubtful. "What you continually fail to realize, dear nephew, is that this machine is inaccurate. As I've said before, I was about to create a regulatory system for it so that a date and time could be specifically calibrated, but I became consumed with other things," he said pointedly.

Griffin remembered that the other "things" his uncle was talking about were his own arrival and the last case they worked on.

"But what if we tried pushing the knob back just a little into where it says 'Past' and not all the way?" Griffin said, indicating the lever on the side of the teapot that pointed to "Past," "Present," and "Future."

Rupert scratched the side of his nose. "I don't know. It might work, but it still could be way off. Remember, you're wanting to arrive at a very specific date and time. It's nearly impossible."

Griffin smiled at his uncle. "But, Uncle, like you said, we have all the *time* in the world. We can keep trying as long as we want, and when we finally hit it, no time will have elapsed."

Rupert smirked. "Good point," he said. And then, just as the waitress was approaching to take their orders, the two clasped hands and Rupert firmly gripped the teapot's handle.

"Ready . . . one, two, THREE!"

And with a flash, the two disappeared from the year 2012 and hurtled back into the past.

The waitress who had been sent to wait on their table happened to be looking down at her mobile phone when the two of them disappeared. She wasn't startled at all when she looked up and noticed that they were gone.

Instead, with a shrug, she continued texting her best friend.

The waitress continued to ignore the impatient stares and frustrated waves of the other restaurant patrons trying to get her attention. She was busy conversing with her friend Tabitha, who had recently bought another Abercrombie & Fitch T-shirt and had had a very unusual experience with two LARPers she'd met on the road near Stonehenge.

It took exactly one thousand one hundred and twenty-three attempts to find the date and time that Griffin had specified to his uncle. In the various tries, Griffin and Rupert had gained a very interesting perspective on the evolution of Baker Street and its surroundings. While traveling back and forth, bumping along through time, they'd encountered a troop of hostile Romans, some wild boars, a close call with a volcanic eruption, and finally, after far too many tries, ended up inside their apartment with exactly five minutes to spare.

Rupert set the teapot down on the table in the kitchen and breathed a sigh of relief. "I really must get started on improving this blasted thing as soon as possible," he said. "It was pure luck that we found this particular time. The odds of doing it again are—"

"Exactly 2.47 billion to one," Griffin whispered, putting a warning finger to his lips and then pointing down the darkened hall. "I had time to figure it out while we were bouncing around. We must be quiet, Uncle. We don't want to alert Miss Pepper to our presence."

Rupert nodded. Griffin could tell his uncle felt as completely exhausted as he did. Rupert tried to pull a dining room chair quietly from the table so that he could sit down, but unfortunately, due to the clutter that was ever present in the flat, the chair's leg banged against a stack of books, sending several thudding to the floor.

Griffin winced. But then he suddenly realized that he recognized the sound! When he'd heard it before, it had been muffled, but it reminded him very much of the sound that he'd heard while upstairs on the night he'd tried to catch the thief.

Next he heard the almost imperceptible pad of his other self's feet upstairs, carefully avoiding the creaky floorboards in his bedroom. With a strange feeling of déjà vu, he peered around the corner from the kitchen and watched as a very familiar figure descended the stairs with his sword cane, looking pale and frightened in the moonlight.

It's me, Griffin thought, feeling amazed. And then, because he was so awestruck, he failed to act as quickly as he'd planned. That was when he heard a rustle and the sound of the front door closing, sounds he remembered hearing from his bedroom on the night of the theft. Recalling how narrowly he'd missed capturing Miss Pepper before, he sprang into action.

"Now!" he said, grabbing his uncle by the sleeve.

"Crikey!" Rupert growled, pausing only to snatch the time-traveling teapot from the table as the two of them leapt into action, chasing after Griffin's own retreating figure.

It's a strange thing to see oneself frightened. But it's an even stranger thing to be the person frightening yourself. As Griffin and Rupert dashed past his own scared figure, Griffin forgot that earlier he'd swung his sword at what he'd thought were agents of Moriarty and had wounded one of them in the process.

The person whose cheek he'd grazed at that moment with the razor-sharp edge of his cane-sword was him!

Griffin let out a cry as the sword whistled past, narrowly missing cutting off his head, and opened a small wound on his cheek. He followed Rupert out the window.

Charlotte Pepper was just dashing behind a building on the corner, and together they chased the lady's retreating shadow through the cobblestone streets, running as fast as they were able.

The Griffin Sharpe who chased Charlotte Pepper thought of his other self at the moment, the one who had now swung his sword at Watts and dented his shiny metal surface. He suddenly wished that he could have talked to his other self and warned him about all that was going to happen and advise him about how he might do things differently.

But alas, their hands were full at present. And unfortunately, because of his hurt leg, Griffin couldn't keep up with his uncle as he chased the retreating figure; he soon fell behind, leaning heavily on his stick for support.

Rupert Snodgrass, on the other hand, was running as fast as his thick legs could carry him, huffing and puffing like a broken-down steam engine.

Maybe it was because he'd grown as accustomed as Griffin to eating Mrs. Tottingham's delicious scones, or perhaps it was because he'd spent much more time in his inventing room than getting regular exercise, but he soon found that a pain had erupted in his side and his once youthful vigor had long since departed.

Breathless and sweating, he chased the lithe figure in boys' clothing down a nearby alleyway.

"Stop . . . you!" he wheezed.

Suddenly, Rupert felt his ankle twist beneath him and he stumbled, crying out as he fell. And then, to his utmost horror, he felt the teapot fly from his outstretched fingers and watched as it soared through the still night air.

"No!" Rupert gasped.

But it was too late.

As Rupert's stocky frame crashed to the cobblestone street, a second crash sounded from not too far away. And it was a sound that Griffin, even though he was lagging behind, couldn't help but identify.

It was the sound of a million tiny pieces of delicate machinery hitting the bricks and the shattering of the pottery that surrounded it. And to Rupert it was the sound of twenty-five years of painstaking labor, methodically creating his own parts from scratch and composing complicated mathematical formulae, gone!

Griffin limped up in time to help his uncle, whose trousers were ripped at the knee, pick up the larger pieces of the destroyed time machine. And as they collected the remains, Rupert said, in a very choky-sounding voice, "Well, that's it, boy. We're ruined."

THE FUTURE DOOR

B ut there must be some way we can fix it," Griffin
said. Rupert stared back at his nephew with a sullen
expression.

"You don't understand, Griffin. This took twenty-five years
to build! I was a young man when I started!" Rupert said.

They sat on the stairs that led up to their apartment. Griffin
stared out at the deserted street, breathing in the cool night air.
His mind raced, trying to figure out another option.

Without the machine, they couldn't return to the time
when they'd left Miss Pepper at Stonehenge and taken the
Chrono-Teleporter.

In the present time they were in right now, Charlotte
Pepper was already en route to deliver the time machine to
Nigel Moriarty in hopes that she could save her sister's life. She
obviously had prearranged transportation and could get there
well before Griffin and his uncle had a chance to follow.

Attempts at finding a new solution raced through Griffin's
head, but he couldn't find a single one that worked. And the

more he thought about all the terrible things that had happened, the more he realized that it all boiled down to one central thing.

The Moriartys' road to power had started with the death of Sherlock Holmes.

If there was some way that we could stop it from happening, all could be set right again.

But they had traveled immediately to Sussex after the teapot had been stolen the first time, and had arrived too late.

No, the only way to prevent Sherlock Holmes from getting murdered at this point was to use the time machine. But if they tried to break into Stonehenge again, he knew that by the time they got there, Moriarty would have already used it. And now, Nigel, realizing that he'd run into Rupert and Griffin in the future, would certainly take measures to protect it with even greater care.

Griffin sighed and rubbed a hand over his forehead. He felt tired, more tired than he'd ever been. His acute mind had never worked so hard on such a complicated problem. He felt that a solution was there, but was just beyond his reach.

What is it, Lord? he prayed. *Please help me think!*

Rupert sat next to him, saying nothing but turning the pieces of his shattered machine over and over in his hands. Griffin noticed the cut beneath the rip in his uncle's trousers and thought about his own bleeding cheek. It was just a scratch, but it hurt.

He wondered if he should knock on their apartment door and ask himself for help.

And that was when it hit him. It was a solution unlike any he'd ever come up with before. It was so bold, and so incredibly unthinkable, that he could do nothing but think that perhaps God had answered his prayer and put it into his mind.

Thank You, he breathed. And then, turning to Snodgrass, he said, "Uncle?"

"Hmm?"

"Is there someplace you know of where you could be safe for a long time? Someplace where nobody could find you?"

Rupert thought for a moment. Then he asked the most obvious question. "How long, exactly?"

Griffin smiled, his teeth cutting a bright semicircle in the moonlight. "Twenty-five years," he said. Then Griffin explained his idea. Rupert stared at him, looking amazed.

"It's unthinkable," he said, stunned.

"But it might work," Griffin replied.

Rupert stood up from the step he'd been sitting on and began to pace.

"You do realize what you're asking? Twenty-five years!" he exclaimed.

"Yes," said Griffin. "It will take a lot of patience. But it should work." He stood and walked down the steps to where his uncle was standing. "If you start building a new time machine now, one that can precisely set a particular date and time . . . then twenty-five years from now you could leave it for me to find. My older self will then use it to return to this time, right here and now! Then we can use the new machine to transport ourselves to the precise time that Moriarty showed up to murder Sherlock Holmes and stop him. It could work!"

Griffin's eyes shone with the possibility. Rupert shook his head, agitated. Griffin could see that for the older man, twenty-five years seemed an eternity!

"But why shouldn't I just use it myself to come back?" Rupert asked. "That way, if anything goes wrong, you won't be at risk."

Griffin put a hand on his uncle's shoulder. "You'll be old. I'll still be relatively young, around forty or so. I'll be able to help us fight Moriarty."

Rupert sighed and ran his fingers through his thinning hair. Then, with a resigned expression, he said, "Well, it is by far the most creative solution to a problem I've ever heard. It might be completely mad, of course. But it certainly is creative."

Then, motioning Griffin to follow, he led him to the side of the stairwell that led up to the apartment. After carefully inspecting the rails that supported the banister, he began to twist one of them, turning it slowly counterclockwise.

"What are you doing?" Griffin asked.

"Long ago . . . [grunt] . . . I knew that a day might come when my inventions and possibly my own person would be in danger. That was . . . [grunt] . . . when I decided to build a safe place where I could remain virtually undetected," Rupert said.

Griffin watched in disbelief as the turning of the rail lowered a false wall, revealing a hidden door beneath the stairwell.

"Behold my 'Future Door,'" Rupert said proudly. "The secret place where I store my most prized possessions. I hoped I would never have to use it as a place to stay, but now I'm very glad I built it."

Rupert produced a small brass key, and Griffin followed his uncle into an amazing, subterranean room filled with every comfort imaginable.

There were kerosene lamps and enough fuel to last well beyond twenty-five years. Griffin stared at massive amounts of carefully stored food, ingeniously preserved and contained by his uncle in sealed metal containers.

There was a rug, sleeping cots, and two comfortable couches. There was even a hearth that, when lit, channeled its smoke through one of the other more conspicuous chimneys in Mrs. Hudson's own ovens.

Of course, the secret quarters were also equipped with an ample supply of tools and engineering supplies so that Rupert could have limitless possibilities for creating his inventions.

"Incredible!" said Griffin. "It's the perfect place! So this is where you hid the Chrono-Teleporter."

"Yes," Rupert said. Then he smiled and gazed around at the comfortable spot. He patted his jacket pocket and removed his notebook.

"Thank goodness I always carry this with me and have the plans to the Snodgrass Chrono-Teleporter written down," he said. Rupert sighed and rubbed a hand through his thinning hair. "But I never thought I'd have to spend time remaking all of the millions of tiny parts. I had to create each one by hand. Crikey! This isn't going to be easy!"

Griffin said, "When do you want to start?"

And Rupert replied, with an uncharacteristic twinkle, "I suppose that there's no better time than the present."

A LONG TIME

Twenty-five years later . . .

For Griffin it was both incredibly long and fantastically short. Many things happened when Rupert Snodgrass began rebuilding his new and improved time machine that first night.

When they started that night, they made sure to leave a note for their other selves on the door at Baker Street, warning them not to knock on the Future Door until twenty-five years later. They didn't want to risk upsetting their plan and had to safeguard against any changes to the current time stream.

Evidently, their other selves got the message, because they were left alone and allowed to do their work.

And it was during those long years that Griffin and his uncle began to learn the true value of patience.

And as the years passed, the world around them was altered profoundly. In their current time, Moriarty had successfully killed Sherlock Holmes, and as a result, he and his infamous cousin gradually assumed control of the entire world. During the first years of his ascent into power, Griffin and his uncle had been able to venture into the streets in relative safety, but as the world under Moriarty's control grew darker and darker, things became progressively more dangerous.

The London they had known and loved changed dramatically. Scarlet banners with a sharp, black *M* emblazoned upon them gradually replaced the Union Jack, Britain's beloved flag. Persons not loyal to the new government were driven underground. Armies of the deadly, crab-like robots Griffin and Rupert had faced beneath Stonehenge swarmed the streets, often attacking innocents and destroying sympathizers of the Crown.

Crime and chaos were everywhere, and in the darkness, members of the Black Widows, the once-secret group of assassins, were now seen on every corner, replacing the comforting sight of the English bobbies who had once protected the city.

But as Griffin grew older, he also became more and more clever. He developed a network of resistance, one that the Moriartys could never catch or stop no matter how hard they tried.

They were vastly outnumbered, but over the years Griffin and his uncle were able to help many of the suffering people, hiding them and giving them shelter as needed.

Year after year, Griffin continued this way, living in a hopeless world but bringing hope wherever he could. He grew wiser and, if possible, even kinder with age . . . but he missed his parents terribly. And because the Moriartys controlled all of the ships, and the mail, and every other possible way of contacting them, Griffin had to suffer quietly and content himself with praying for them every night before he went to sleep.

But twenty-five years doesn't last forever, and one impossible day, twenty-five years later, an aged and wrinkled Rupert Snodgrass stood up from his workbench. In his hand he held a gleaming new time machine and pronounced, with a shaky, tired voice, "It's done, boy. It's finally done."

Now, time is a funny thing, for while this twenty-five-year journey was happening, another version of reality was happening too. Many scientists believe that time runs in streams, like train tracks traveling in parallel lines. And on very rare occasions, it is theoretically possible that these timelines could converge.

So it was that mere seconds after Rupert Snodgrass began building his new time machine, Griffin both was and was not startled by a gentle knock on the door. He wasn't startled because he'd expected it to happen and was pleased to find that his plan had worked. But he was also startled by the thought of meeting the person on the other side of the door.

Rupert continued to build, following the carefully drawn plans in his notebook, as Griffin cautiously approached what his uncle called his "Future Door." And as it turned out, that name described it perfectly.

As it swung back on its hinges, a man in his late thirties with blond hair, still a bit shaggy, stared down at his younger self with the same sad, blue eyes they both possessed. They both leaned on ebony canes and had matching scars on their cheeks. Griffin's was still new, while the other had faded into a very thin, white line.

"Hello, Griffin," the visitor said in a deep voice. It was a gentle voice filled with kindness, but not without a smile in it.

And Griffin, extending his hand, approached his older self and said, "Hello, Mr. Sharpe. So glad you could come!"

THE SPIDER AND THE BEE

Nigel Moriarty gazed at the beautiful English garden, not noticing the particular flowers or the carefully ordered beehives. He was there for one purpose and one purpose only, to eliminate his and his cousin's chief rival once and for all.

Holmes shouldn't have survived the Reichenbach Falls, the waterfall that many years ago should have claimed both his and the professor's lives. It had been a ferocious duel of wits, one that culminated in a physical fight that had sent both men plunging to their doom.

But they were special men, Moriarty thought. *Survivors.*

He had been able to rescue his uncle's twisted body from the rocks below and build for him a life support system, a chair that would supply him with the ability to function once more. Even though his uncle's body was wrecked, his mind was intact, and that was all that mattered.

But Sherlock Holmes had escaped injury, and that had only inflamed the cousins' desire for revenge. It seemed that the man people called "the Great Detective" couldn't be killed. He always lived to fight another day, was always one step ahead of his opponents.

"Until today," Nigel Moriarty whispered.

He lifted his hand to reveal the sparkling, spider-shaped ring on his finger. Atrax, in her death, had supplied him with the perfect weapon to take the life from their opponent forever. How fitting that it was a spider among Holmes's bees, two creatures with the ability to sting one another, each relying upon the advantage of who struck first.

Moriarty crept up the garden pathway, knowing exactly where Holmes would be. The book had told him enough about what was to come, and he'd deduced the rest. For the first time in history, the great Sherlock Holmes would be caught unawares, and after this moment, history would be changed forever.

And the future would be left to the Moriartys.

The lean figure in white contrasted sharply with the black-cloaked figure that approached silently from behind. The buzzing of the hives drowned out Moriarty's footsteps as he inched closer and closer, his hand outstretched, the needle poised to strike.

And then, from out of nowhere, three figures emerged. The first two, a boy and an older man, dove from behind the rows of white beehives and tackled the detective.

In the split second he saw them, Moriarty knew who they were: Griffin Sharpe and that meddling Snodgrass! But the third figure he didn't recognize, though he somehow seemed incredibly familiar.

All of this registered in a split second, for Nigel Moriarty was soon distracted by a second surprise, and this one occupied his attention to a much greater degree.

There was a blinding flash as something silver reflected the summer sunlight. A second later he felt the sting from an all-too-familiar blade.

It was the same blade he'd once used on an innocent young man who had disrupted his plans.

Griffin Sharpe had survived its deadly blow.

But Nigel Moriarty would not. As he gazed at the face of his attacker, he took in the eyes and knew at once who it was. It didn't seem possible. He was older, much older, but those were the same blue eyes, now filled with an even deeper sadness than they'd had within them on the face of a child.

"How?" was all he managed to say before he crumpled to the ground.

And it was the last word that Nigel Moriarty ever said.

NO PLACE LIKE HOLMES

Young Griffin Sharpe, Rupert Snodgrass, and the older Griffin Sharpe sat with Sherlock Holmes and Dr. Watson at 221B Baker Street, enjoying a much-needed cup of tea.

The older Rupert Snodgrass had refused to travel back in time with them to save Sherlock Holmes. The old fellow had said that he intended to take a very long and much-deserved rest. And Griffin couldn't blame him at all. After all, his uncle had been working on his invention for nearly twenty-five years without a break!

"Needless to say, I am eternally grateful to you all," the great detective said. "You have done me a great service, and I'm in your debt."

"It is good to have you back, sir," Rupert Snodgrass said. And to his surprise, he found that he actually meant it. "I really don't think that this apartment should belong to anyone else."

"It does feel like home," Dr. Watson commented, glancing around at the familiar surroundings. A fire blazed in the hearth, and the pungent but oddly comforting smell of pipe tobacco and chemicals from Holmes's experiments hung in the air.

"As for Charlotte Pepper and her young sister, I have already arranged for the girls' release. The Black Widows were very reluctant to have their London whereabouts publicized and, with the death of Nigel, have returned to hiding," Holmes said, smiling. "I also managed the release of Mr. H. G. Wells and the rest of Moriarty's prisoners from the dungeons beneath the Tower of London."

He turned to Rupert, who was sipping his tea. "By the way, Snodgrass. Miss Pepper asked about you."

Rupert Snodgrass sat up so abruptly in his chair he nearly spilled his tea.

"She did?" he asked.

"Yes. She said something about hoping that you can forgive her for the theft of your invention and would enjoy an opportunity for conversation at a later date, if you were so inclined."

Rupert blushed deep crimson. In reply, he muttered something like, "Delightful woman. Pleasure's mine."

Watson chuckled, then, turning to Sherlock Holmes, said, "So, you've really decided to come out of retirement at your age, Holmes? Are you certain you want to do this? After all, you're no spring chicken anymore."

"Begging your pardon, old chap, but this old rooster still has quite a bit of fight left in him," Holmes quipped, then added seriously, "I'm quite certain, Watson. My presence is still needed on Baker Street as demonstrated by the clever rescue that was orchestrated by our young friend here." He indicated Griffin with a nod. "Although the younger Moriarty is no longer a problem, his uncle certainly remains so."

Dr. Watson gave young Griffin a friendly wink and passed him a plate of Mrs. Tottingham's famous scones. But for the first time in his life, Griffin wasn't hungry for them.

He felt glad that Sherlock Holmes's life had been spared and that he was back where he belonged, protecting London from evil. But he felt deeply troubled by the fact that Nigel Moriarty's death had come by his own hand, even if it was by the hand of his older self.

Killing someone was not a Christian thing to do. How, then, could he have been capable of ending another's life, even if Nigel was one of the most evil men in London?

The older Griffin gazed at his younger self, reading his thoughts. Then the man stood up from the table and asked, "Would you like to go for a walk?"

Griffin still didn't make eye contact, but nodded his head. After excusing himself, he slid from the table and walked with his older self out of Sherlock Holmes's apartment and onto Baker Street, both of their ebony canes keeping time with each other as they walked.

The sun was setting, casting gentle shadows over the tall buildings. The *clip-clop* of a few horses' hooves pulling hansom cabs echoed on the cobblestones, but other than that, the street was empty.

Young Griffin gazed at the street, his sad, blue eyes reflecting the troubling question that he couldn't bring himself to ask. After a long pause the older man cleared his throat and said gently, "You're wondering if there was another way."

Griffin didn't say anything. When the older man spoke again, his voice was still gentle but also firm. "No. There wasn't."

Griffin looked sharply up. "But there had to be. It was some-one's life!"

Older Griffin gazed down at him and sighed. "You know the way we think. Once our uncle finished building the time machine, I used it to explore every possible scenario."

"How was that possible?" asked Griffin.

Older Griffin glanced back up at the darkening street and said, "I asked Rupert to create one last enhancement to the machine, a setting that would allow me to hop along the millions of different time streams as an observer."

He glanced at Griffin. "Imagine the ability to watch endless scenarios unfold based on the different choices you would make. To see the cause and effect of every decision and never age a day while watching them!"

His voice grew quiet. "Rupert was able to make it work. He really is a genius. I think he called the invention his 'Snodgrass Time Stream Synchronizer' or something like that."

Griffin listened, awestruck. His older self continued, speaking slowly.

"I watched as I tried every possible way to stop Moriarty without killing him. The trouble was, no matter how hard I tried to find a different outcome, every time it turned out the same. Millions of possibilities . . . and I tried every single one."

He sighed. "One time I tried capturing Nigel Moriarty, but later he escaped. Another time I used the Scorpion to teleport him somewhere else . . . of course, he found his way back into power again. Every scenario, every timeline, ended with the same result. I tried hundreds of times to keep Charlotte Pepper from stealing the machine, and yet it still happened. I tried persuading Rupert Snodgrass to never build it, and yet it still was made. Sometimes by him, sometimes by someone else. But no matter what I tried, Nigel Moriarty stole it and had countless innocents murdered, and his way into power always hinged on the death of Sherlock Holmes."

Older Griffin gazed back out to the streets, and Younger Griffin noticed the lines around the older man's eyes. They were eyes that looked like they had seen too much.

"If one evil man has to die so that countless innocents can live, then there is no alternative," the man said. Then he looked back down at Griffin, and when their eyes met, young Griffin was surprised to see the tears in the older man's eyes.

"But taking a life, no matter whose it is, is always a terrible thing."

They stood in silence for some time, each lost in his own thoughts. The words his older self said made sense to Griffin, but he had a hard time accepting them. Perhaps he would better understand when he was older, he decided. But then he wondered if he ever really would.

The sun sank below the horizon, and the gaslights on Baker Street came on one by one, each lit by a lamplighter and his young assistant.

Griffin noticed their matching, ragged clothes, counted the number of missing buttons on each of their coats, and calculated the difference in their sizes. And he realized that their body sizes were not that different from the size difference between himself and the older version that stood beside him.

He gazed up at his older self and felt that he had many unanswered questions. He took a deep breath and said, "What will happen now? Moriarty has been stopped and we fixed the future. Doesn't that mean that the version of you that I'm talking to shouldn't exist? How is it possible that you're still here? Did my uncle invent something that would keep you, you? And you said that you've seen all the different timelines. If that's so, what will happen to us in this one? What will I be like five years from now, or ten years? Will I grow up and get married? What about my parents and Uncle Rupert? How long will they live? How long will I live? Is there anything I need to watch out for? Will I really become the World's Most Secret Detective?"

Older Griffin smiled down at his younger self, his teeth shining bright in the gathering gloom. "Do you really want to know?"

Griffin paused to think. Here he was, with an opportunity to have answers to any questions he wanted to ask. Should he do it?

He had an inquisitive mind, a mind that noticed everything. As long as he could remember, he had sought the answers to his questions, and the more difficult and puzzling, the better.

But now, as he gazed up at the same pair of sad, blue eyes he himself possessed, he found that for the first time he didn't want to know.

"It would spoil the adventure, wouldn't it?"

And as the older Griffin put his arm around the shoulder of his younger self, he laughed, and Griffin knew exactly what he was going to say.

"Couldn't have said it better myself," the two of them said at the same time. And then they both went back inside Sherlock Holmes's apartment, each walking with the help of his ebony cane, to help themselves to as many of Mrs. Tottingham's famous scones as they could possibly eat.

EPILOGUE

G riffin's determination to become the World's Most Secret Detective only grew stronger as the years went by. And that is why, dear reader, none of the things he's done have ever been written down until this point.

The years went by, and Griffin grew older, but whenever a crime was solved, he gave the police the credit and never gave his name to the press.

It couldn't be helped that a few of the great criminals knew about him, like Professor Moriarty and the Black Widows, but most of the evildoers didn't. And that was why Griffin was able to catch so many, and how he ended up saving our entire planet from destruction more than thirteen times.

And although he is currently well over a hundred years old, he still goes on doing the same thing.

Oh, didn't I tell you? Griffin remains one of four people who tasted the water from the Fountain of Youth.

But that is another story. I have said enough. I express eternal gratitude to Mr. Sharpe and his daughter, Dame Victoria, for allowing me to tell two of his tales, and until allowed to do otherwise, I shall remain silent. For, if Griffin was able to remain humble and fade into obscurity, so too shall I.

Thank you for reading.

HOW SHARPE ARE YOU?

See how many of these questions you can get right without looking back in the book. Here's your rating system:

1 TO 3 CORRECT: You'd make a good Baker Street Irregular, one of Sherlock Holmes's assistants.

4 TO 7 CORRECT: Scotland Yard police inspectors will be keeping their eye on you.

8 TO 9 CORRECT: Rupert Snodgrass would be jealous. Good job!

PERFECT 10: You're the next Griffin Sharpe. Well done!

1. In the very beginning of the book, what meal was Mrs. Hudson preparing?
2. In what city did Griffin's parents live?
3. Name three of the inventions listed in Rupert Snodgrass's notebook.
4. What was Charlotte Pepper's sister's name?
5. What do some people believe Stonehenge was?

6. When Griffin and his uncle traveled to the future, what Bible reference did Griffin look up in the bookstore?
7. In the future, what was Sherlock Holmes's apartment turned into?
8. What creature did Nigel Moriarty run into when he first used the time machine?
9. What happened to Griffin's cheek?
10. Who was the man who helped Rupert develop his time machine? Hint: He was kidnapped by Moriarty.

GRIFFIN SHARPE
MINI -MYSTERIES

THE CASE OF THE
BIG GAME HUNTER

A Griffin Sharpe Mini-Mystery

Griffin Sharpe sat quietly in his theater box seat, waiting for the show to begin. He was excited to hear the lecture, a speech by the notable explorer and world traveler Sir Henry Moss! All who were in attendance had heard of the incredible hunting trophies Moss had brought back from exotic countries, many of which were housed in the British Museum.

The idea of hunting didn't appeal much to Griffin. He hated to see anything killed. But like most boys his age, he loved adventure, and the legend of Henry Moss was well-known to him even back home in America. The famous Moss had been to the deepest jungles, navigated impossible rivers, and faced all kinds of danger in places that nobody had ever ventured to explore. Griffin had read all about him in the Penny Dreadfuls, the nickname for inexpensive magazines filled with sensational stories, and could recite each of Moss's adventures from memory, often boring his uncle with his obsession over the details.

The special event was by invitation only, and Griffin had been delighted when Sherlock Holmes had passed along two tickets to him and Rupert, claiming that he had a very serious case that was taking up his attention.

Suddenly, the footlights on the stage grew brighter, and a round of applause thundered around the auditorium. Griffin clapped as loudly as everyone else, his eyes shining with excitement.

A rotund man with a very bushy beard introduced Sir Henry Moss, stating "that he had done more to further exploration and protect the British Empire than Admiral Nelson himself," which was no small claim. Everyone knew that Admiral Nelson was the greatest British hero who ever lived!

Seconds later, a tall man with very distinguished side-whiskers took the stage, to more thunderous applause. Griffin noted that he wore a pith helmet, a tawny-colored jacket, and heavy explorer's boots. To his delight, Griffin saw that he looked exactly like the illustrations of him that he had seen in the magazines!

The applause died down, and Sir Henry Moss launched into one of his harrowing tales.

"It was on a blistering day in Zimbabwe that my companions and I approached a nearly impassible river. The banks of the Limpopo had been almost entirely swallowed by the rushing, swirling water, due to a torrential downpour a few days before."

Sir Henry's glittering black eyes scanned the crowd, noticing that all were riveted to his every word. Griffin squirmed with excitement as he spoke, thrilled to be hearing this story firsthand. It was one that he hadn't read about in any of his massive collection of Penny Dreadfuls.

"I had managed to kill a ferocious lion a few hours before, and felt certain that the rest of the pride would soon hunt me down. Unless we traversed the river, there would be little hope of throwing them off the scent. We were, in effect, doomed!" Sir Henry Moss said.

He paused for effect. "With no apparent way across the churning river, we were left with little hope. Suddenly, a series of loud roars sounded in the jungle not fifty paces behind me. I drew my pistol, having recently lost my elephant gun in a stampede of wildebeests. This was it! I would make my stand, taking down as many as I could before the inevitable happened."

The crowd hung on every word. The entire theater was silent.

"But then, just as all seemed lost, I spotted a small herd of giraffe grazing nearby." Sir Henry Moss smiled, showing rows of glittering white teeth.

"Now, the giraffe is a creature especially suited to crossing bodies of water, due to its extended neck, and they are quite excellent swimmers. So after working with my guides to surround a few of the docile beasts, we were able to make it across in short order, just as the pride of lions appeared."

He raised his palm to his forehead in a theatrical gesture, pretending to wipe sweat from his eyes. "By Jove, it was a relief to escape the ferocious beasts. Their frustrated roars split the air, shaking the very trees to their roots. After landing on the opposite bank, I was so delighted by our harrowing escape that I fired off three rounds in a victory salute, sending the big pussy-cats running for cover."

He sighed and opened his arms in a wide gesture. "It was one of my narrower escapes, to be sure," he finished.

The crowd cheered. Sir Henry Moss bowed. Rupert, who was sitting next to Griffin, grinned at him, impressed like everyone else at the incredible ingenuity Moss had shown in escaping the great cats.

But Griffin didn't share his uncle's enthusiasm. He stared at the posturing man onstage, his face twisted in an attitude of stunned disbelief.

"What's wrong?" asked Rupert, looking confused.

"He's a fake," Griffin said quietly. Then added, "I really shouldn't have wasted my pennies on those magazines."

How did Griffin know?

Turn to page 209 for the answer.

THE CASE OF THE
MISSING MASTERPIECE

A Griffin Sharpe Mini-Mystery

G riffin Sharpe gazed at the incredible paintings, taking in every detail and appreciating every brushstroke. Paris was absolutely beautiful, and its collection of art even more so. The Louvre Museum was the last stop on his vacation, a wonderful treat provided by his parents.

Griffin's mother and father had taken a steamship to London to visit their son and to announce the happy news. His father had received special permission from the Methodist Church to temporarily pastor a small country church in England. It meant that Griffin and his uncle Rupert could continue to work on cases together for a little while longer, something that made Griffin feel quite happy. He hoped that it would be several months before his family would return to Boston. He'd grown accustomed to life in London and would miss his routines, especially his frequent visits to Mrs. Tottingham's bakery!

"Look, Mother," Griffin said excitedly. "That line over there is for the *Mona Lisa!*"

Mrs. Sharpe gazed down at her son, her eyes twinkling. "Well, we mustn't miss that one. Lead on, dear."

Griffin took his place in line with his parents right behind. He gazed at his printed brochure, noting the important details surrounding the famous painting.

"Did you know that in the 1800s the *Mona Lisa* hung in Napoleon's bedroom?" Griffin asked his father.

Mr. Sharpe, who was in the middle of eating a delicious-looking French pastry, swallowed and said, "Is that so?"

"Yes!" said Griffin excitedly. "I just read it here."

He paged through the small brochure, eagerly soaking in the details as the line slowly inched toward the painting.

"Oh, and how about this?" Griffin said. "Leonardo da Vinci never sold the portrait to the family who commissioned it. In fact, he never sold the painting at all!"

Griffin's parents were used to their son's excitement over learning something new and listened patiently as the line wound back and forth through the long rows of paintings. Finally, after almost two hours, they reached the viewing area.

Behind velvet ropes was the masterpiece. Griffin's breath caught in his throat as he gazed at the beautiful, serene woman in the painting. He took in the famous expression, her knowing glance, her eyebrows slightly lifted to give way to her gentle smile.

But the reason his breath caught wasn't because Griffin was awed over her beauty. He glanced back down at the brochure, noting the reproduction of the painting enclosed therein. Then he folded up the brochure and put it in his pocket.

He turned to his father and said, "I think we'd better notify the police."

Griffin's parents stared back down at him, concerned.

"Why? What happened?" they asked simultaneously.

"Because," Griffin said as he marched toward the French security guard standing nearby, "the *Mona Lisa* has been stolen!"

How did Griffin know?

Turn to page 209 for the answer.

HOW TO BREW THE PERFECT POT OF BRITISH TEA

E ver wonder how they do it in Britain? This is the perfect technique for a wonderful pot of tea. Don't forget the scones!

1. The proper way to brew a cup of tea is to start with boiling water. This is essential! Don't just heat the water . . . boil it!

2. The tea bag should be placed in the cup or pot before the water is added, not afterward. The water has to be at the boiling point when it makes contact with the tea or it will not brew properly.

3. Make sure the cup or pot is nice and hot *before* you start. You can rinse the cup or pot with hot water and keep it covered while the water is coming to a boil.

4. Leave the bag in the water for at least two to three minutes, depending on how strong you like it. And don't "bob" the bag up and down while you wait. Your patience will be rewarded!

5. English Breakfast is a good tea to use in America. Twinings is a popular brand.

6. If you take your tea with milk, put the milk in the cup first and then pour the tea over it. If you like sugar, use white sugar, not brown. One lump or two? It's your choice!

7. Sit back and enjoy your cup while reading about Griffin Sharpe's adventures. Of course, a nice plate filled with Mrs. Tottingham's Lemon Scones is the perfect companion while you drink! (You can find that recipe in the first book about Griffin Sharpe, *No Place Like Holmes.*) Enjoy!

ANSWERS TO GRIFFIN SHARPE
MINI-MYSTERIES

ANSWER TO "THE CASE OF THE BIG GAME HUNTER"
Giraffes don't swim and will always refuse to cross large bodies of water, including rivers.

ANSWER TO "THE CASE OF THE MISSING MASTERPIECE"
When Griffin noticed the *Mona Lisa*'s eyebrows, he knew the painting to be a fake. The real *Mona Lisa* doesn't have any, and she doesn't have eyelashes either!

Travel back in time to London and solve mysteries with Sherlock Holmes's protégé!

Griffin Sharpe notices everything, which makes him the perfect detective! And since he lives next door to Sherlock Holmes, mysteries always seem to find him. With Griffin's keen mind and strong faith, together with his uncle Rupert's genius inventions, there is no case too tricky for the detectives of 221 Baker Street!

By Jason Lethcoe

www.tommynelson.com
www.jasonlethcoe.com/holmes

Check out all of the great books in the series!

No Place Like Holmes ❖ *The Future Door*